Larry Marder's
BEANWORLD

A most peculiar comic book experience!

D1809557

Characters not
shown actual size!

Book Three

1

ISBN 1-887245-02-2

Cover color:	Liz Lewis
Book design:	Doug Griffith
Book Production Manager:	Ronna Vladic
Beanworld Press CFO:	Corinne Marder

Larry Marder's Beanworld: Book Three is published by The Beanworld Press, Inc., 363 Whitecap Lane, Newport Coast, CA 92657. Beanworld is ® and © 1997 Larry Marder. No unauthorized reproduction allowed except for limited portions for review or other journalistic purposes. All rights reserved.

Printed in Canada. First printing

Dedicated
to the memory
of my little brother,
Jon.

I miss you every day, kid.
Larry

BEANWORLD PRIMER

 This is **Chow** The **Beans** eat it. The **Hoi-Polloi** use it for money.

The **Beans** live a happy idyllic life beneath the guidance of **Gran'Ma'Pa**; their rhythmic spiritual and culinary guardian.

 Sometimes a **Sprout-Butt** falls from **Gran'Ma'Pa.** **Mr. Spook** always tries to snag it on the first bounce.

 The **Chow Sol'jers** are on the march! Over the **Legendary Edge** they go!

 They splash into the **Thin Lake,** sink through the **Four Realities** and **Bone Zone** to emerge in the noisy crowded territory of the greedy, gambling **Hoi-Polloi Ring Herd.**

BEANS ARE HERE TO STEAL OUR CHOW.

The **Hoi-Polloi** form partnership **Rings** in order to protect their wealth. But the **Beans** are clever and know how to exploit the **Ring's** weaknesses.

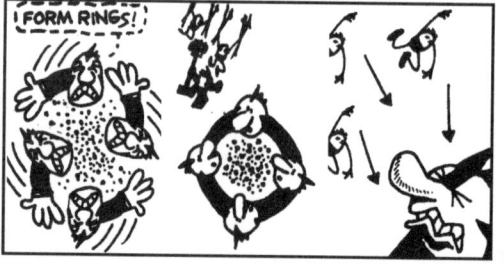

FORM RINGS!

PLUK! PLUK! PLUK! PLUK! PLUK!

The **Beans** break the **Ring,** steal the **Chow** and flee! The **Sprout-Butt** is left behind to heal the hurting **Hoi-Polloi.**

The wounded paupers form a new **Ring** and begin to sing sweet love songs to the **Sprout-Butt.**

The **Sprout-Butt** dances and grows. Eventually it explodes and turns itself into a new batch of **Chow.**

The **Hoi-Polloi** divide the new **Chow** and resume their gambling.

WE WAIT UNTIL GRAN'MA'PA DROPS A SPROUT-BUTT BEFORE WE RAID.

THE SPROUT-BUTT PAYS FOR THE CHOW WE STEAL.

THE LIFE GRAN'MA'PA PROVIDES IS PERFECT AS LONG AS WE EACH DO OUR JOBS.

The **Chow Sol'jers** return to the **Beanworld.** They drop their plunder into the **Chowdown Pool.** The **Beans** soak up as much food as each desires.

CONTENTS

WHAT HAPPENED IN BOOK ONE.

One day, something terrible happened! A vicious enemy, the **Army of the Mirthful Mossy Mammoth**, invaded the **Beanworld.**

The enemy **Army** cooked, killed and canned many of the **Hoi-Polloi Ring Herd**. It was terrible!

Fortunately for the **Beans, Gran'Ma'Pa** provided an awesome weapon: **The Flip-Flop Tool.**

Mr. Spook was brave and the enemy **Army** was wiped out.

The **Hoi-Polloi** gave the **Beans** a mountain of **Chow** as a reward.

Too much Chow! Beanworld became unbalanced. The **Beans** forgot how to work. The **Hoi-Polloi** forgot how to play.

> ALL WE DO IS EAT & SLEEP.

> WE'RE BORED.

> I CARE TO WAGER SOME CHOW?

> WHY BOTHER?

All understood that the problem was the abundance of **Chow** but no one knew the proper way to get rid of the surplus.

> WE COULD DUMP IT IN THE THIN LAKE...

> BUT IT'S WRONG TO WASTE FOOD.

From out of **Der Stinkle, Der Kveen** and some creepy **bugs** got wise to the mountain of **Chow,** ate the whole thing, laid eggs and died.

Meanwhile , **Professor Garbanzo** was frustrated by her inability to successfully invent a **Twink** tool.

One of the **Chow Sol'jers** began to act strange. He played in **Proffy's Twink Trash.** Soon he broke out and became **Beanish,** the creator of the **Fabulous Look • See • Show!**

When **Twinks** are in the proximity of a **Mystery Pod,** a metamorphosis occurs. Both objects are transformed into something new and potent: **The Float Factor!**

Also, **Professor Garbanzo** reminisced about the unhappy days before **Mr. Spook** had his trusty **fork** to sweeten a **Sprout-Butt** on the first bounce.

The **Sprout-Butts** used to be ill-tempered. This did not please the **Hoi-Polloi.** They abused the **Sprout-Butts** to replace their assets. The result was foul tasting **Chow.**

One day **Mr. Spook** helped a wounded **Big Fish.** He was rewarded with a shiny new **fork.**

Mr. Spook didn't like the **fork** until the **fork's Sprout-Butt**-sweetening-snagging-action was discovered. This led to great tasting **Chow,** the building of the **Chowdown Pool** and the discovery of the joys of group dining.

WHAT HAPPENED IN BOOK TWO.

One day while sketching using the **Float Force,** **Beanish** made an accidental discovery.

From that day forward, each day at midday **Beanish** went to go visit his mysterious friend.

There was only one rule he had to keep.

THE BEANWORLD GLOSSARY

BEANISH — Artist. Creator of the Fabulous•Look•See•Show.

BONE ZONE — Skull remains of Hoi-Polloi ring herd slaughtered in Beanworld: Book One.

BOOM'R BAND — A hot trio of Beanworld musicians.

CHOW — A dark, stony substance. The beans eat it and the Hoi-Polloi use it for money.

CHOWDOWN — The act of consuming food.

CHOWDOWN POOL — Giant tub used by the beans as a communal feeding place.

CHOW SOL'JER ARMY — They steal chow from the Hoi-Polloi. Mr. Spook is the leader of the two divisions: the spear fling'n flank'rs and the Chow Pluk'rs.

DREAMISHNESS — Beanish's secret friend and muse.

GOOFY SERVICE JERKS — Reproductive propellant delivery service.

GRAN'MA'PA — Beanworld's spiritual and culinary guardian. sole source of Sprout-Butts.

GUNK'L'DUNK — All purpose adhesive.

FLOAT FACTOR — When Twinks get near mystery pods, both objects transform into a new entity that floats in the air.

THE FOUR REALITIES — (Slats, Hoops, Twinks & Chips) easily obtainable raw materials for Beanworld industry (for example, a slat and a chip are manufactured into a spear).

HOI-POLLOI RING HERD — Greedy, gambling folk. The only creatures with the ability to process Sprout-Butts into chow. General adversaries to the beans.

THE LEGENDARY EDGE — departure point for trips to the Four Realities and below.

NOTWORMS — What Mr. Spook's fork is made of. Also called Tu'ba'lu Squib'r'ish.

POD'L'POOL — The gift. The home of the baby beans

POD'L'POOL CUTIES — The baby beans

PROFESSOR GARBANZO — Toolmaker and thinker.

PROVERBIAL SANDY BEACH — Re-entry point from trips to the Four Realities and below.

MR. SPOOK — Hero and leader of the Chow Sol'jer Army.

MYSTERY PODS — Powerful objects of unknown origin. Used in the Float Factor.

SPROUT BUTT — Vocal off-shoot of Gran'ma'pa. Hoi-Polloi convert Sprout-Butts into chow.

THIN LAKE — Fresh water that covers the Four Realities.

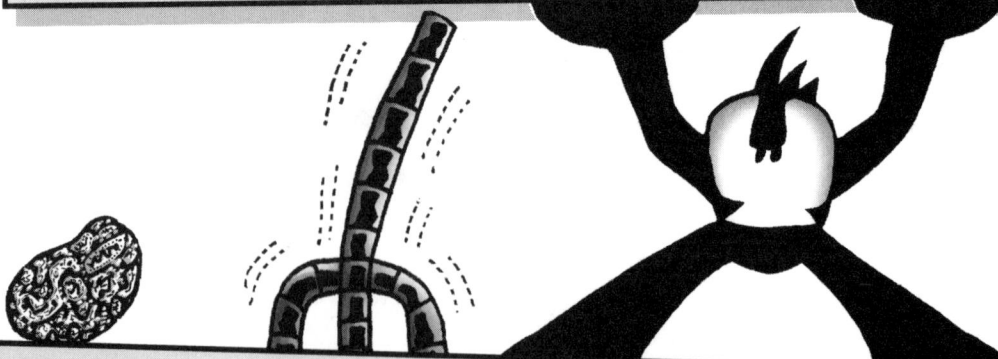

ONE CAUTION. Please don't look for scientific or magical explanations, you won't find any. **Beanworld** is a separate reality. It's not just a *place,* it's a *process!* It is what it is and th-that's all folks!

Deep down; down deep!

BEANISH
has a secret
power.

Larry Marder
©1987

WHAT WAS **THAT** ALL ABOUT?

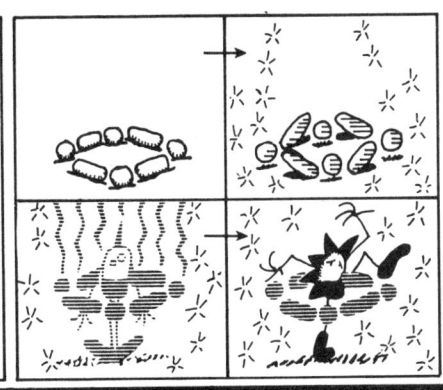

WOW! I JUST REALIZED HOW MUCH THOSE "JERKS" LOOKED LIKE **MR. SPOOK'S TRUSTY FORK!**

I WONDER WHAT THAT MEANS?

I BETTER GO ASK PROFESSOR GARBANZO!

WHAT AM I THINKING? **I CAN'T CONSULT PROFFY!**

THAT WOULD BE A **CONTRACT VIOLATION:**

YOUR SECRET ABILITY TO VISIT ME IS A GREAT POWER, BEANISH!

BUT YOU MUST NEVER, EVER TELL ANYONE ABOUT ME.

IF YOU DO, YOU WILL NEVER, EVER SEE ME AGAIN.

DO YOU UNDERSTAND WHAT I'M SAYING, BEANISH?

yes...

It takes tremendous self control not to speak of such amazing adventures. Fortunately the <u>intensity</u> of the experience fades quickly upon return to the <u>real world</u>, the BEANWORLD.

AAGH!!

MY SECRET POWER IS SOOOOOO **FRUSTRATING** SOMETIMES.

I'M HUNGRY...

FOOD is on the way! At this very moment MR. SPOOK and the CHOW SOL'JER ARMY are taking care of business with their adversaries, the HOI-POLLOI RING HERD!

BEANS ARE HERE TO STEAL OUR CHOW!

SPEAR FLING'N FLANK'RS MOVE INTO POSITION!

WE'RE ON OUR WAY, MR. SPOOK!

FIRST WE **FLANK!**

THIS IS GONNA BE VERY PAINFUL!

THEN WE **FLING!**

LET'S TRY THE **NEW** ROUTINE MR. SPOOK TAUGHT US!

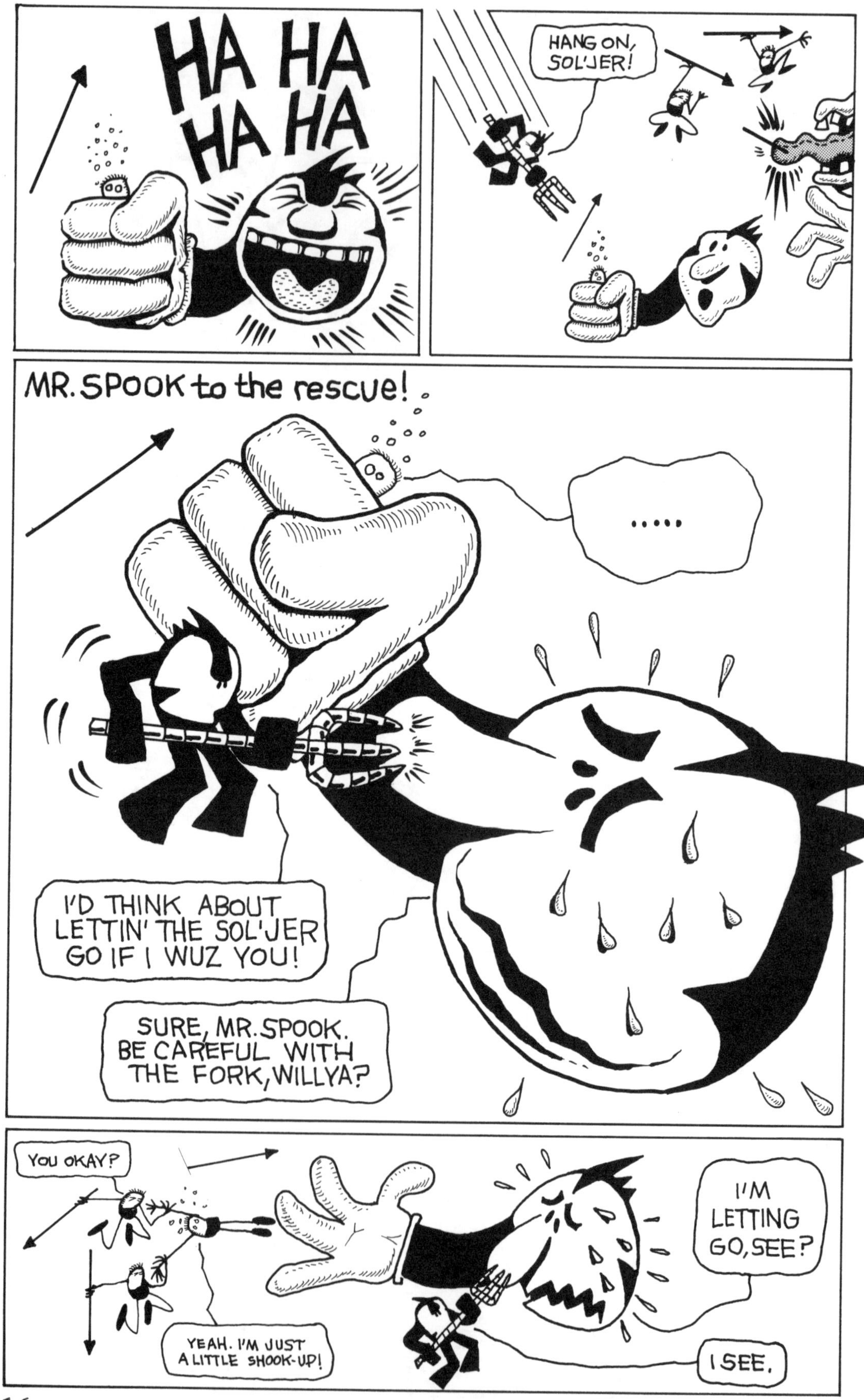

HA HA HA HA

HANG ON, SOL'JER!

MR. SPOOK to the rescue!

.....

I'D THINK ABOUT LETTIN' THE SOL'JER GO IF I WUZ YOU!

SURE, MR. SPOOK. BE CAREFUL WITH THE FORK, WILLYA?

YOU OKAY?

YEAH. I'M JUST A LITTLE SHOOK-UP!

I'M LETTING GO, SEE?

I SEE.

HERE'S YOUR "THANK YOU!"

The HOI-POLLOI RING has been **smashed!** The CHOW PLUK'RS sweep in to grab the CHOW while the HOI-POLLOI are reeling from their injuries.

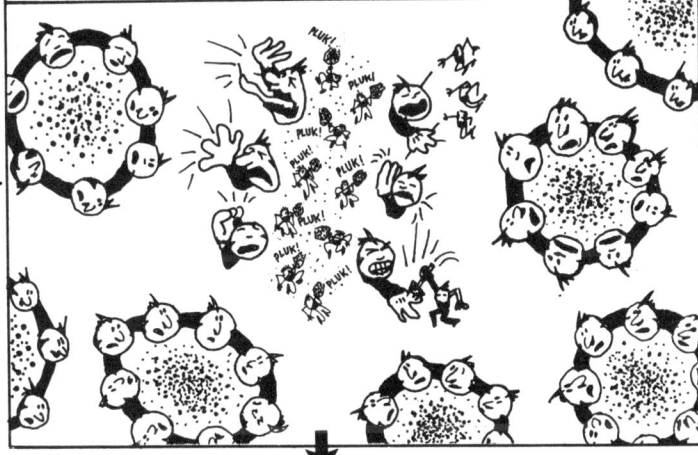

PLUK! PLUK! PLUK! PLUK! PLUK!

PLUK!

THE **NEW** SPEAR FLING'R TACTICAL MANEUVER PERFORMED **WAY TOO WELL.**

PLUK'N WANDS filled, the CHOW SOL'JER ARMY withdraws..

THE FLING INTO THE SOFT PART CREATED TOO MUCH BLIND THRASHING!

17

The CHOW SOL'JERS are home!
The BOOM'R BAND jams the song of safe return.

PLUK'N WANDS ARE BULGING TODAY!

WHERE'S PROFFY?

SHE'S WORKING LATE, MR. SPOOK.

NOT AGAIN!

PROFFY'S WORKING TOO HARD. SHE'S GOTTA LEARN TO RELAX!

PROFESSOR GARBANZO is in *ecstasy.*

AW NO, NOT MORE MYSTERY POD INVENTIONS!

ORDER OUT OF CHAOS!

The CHOWDOWN POOL.

20

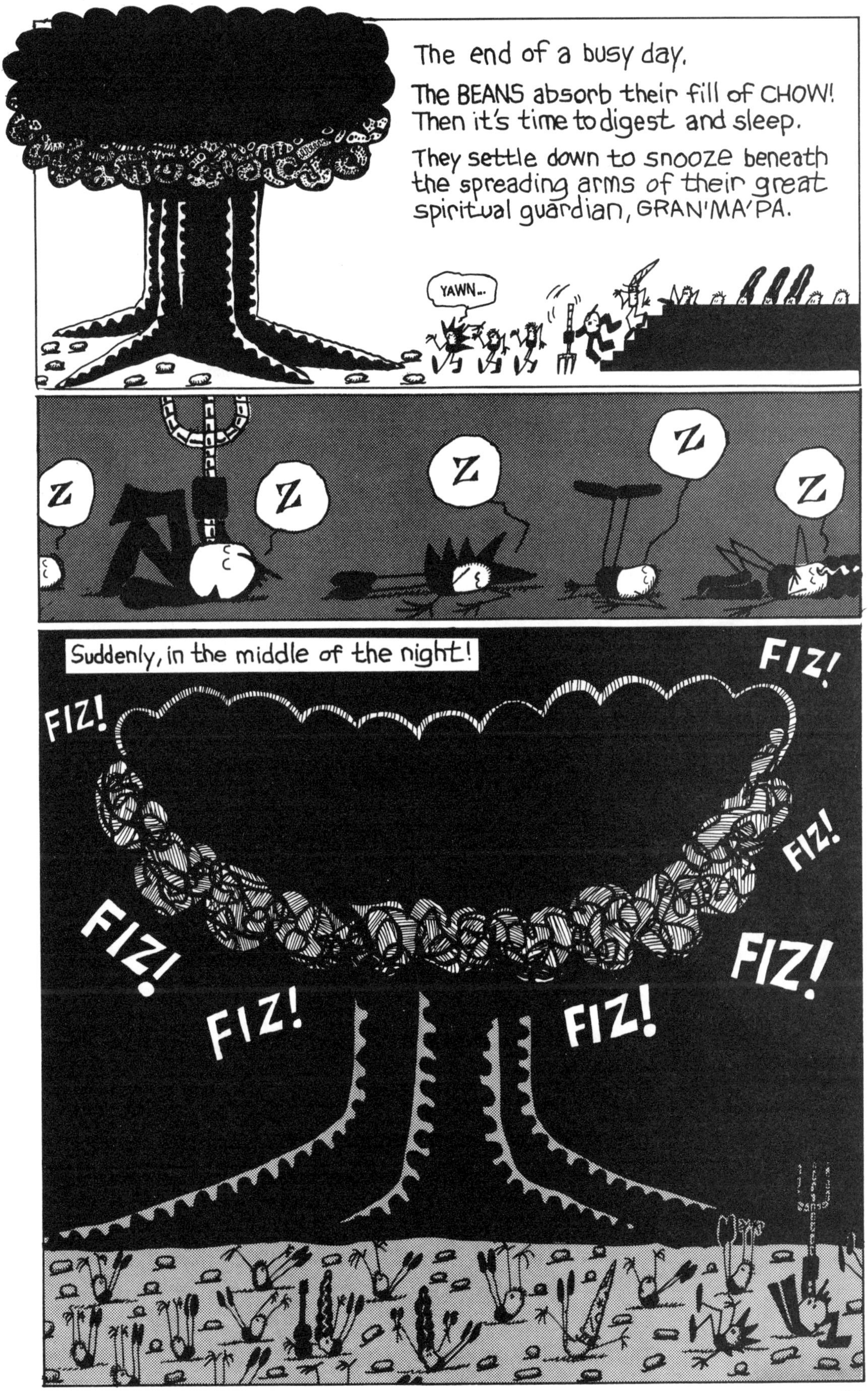

The end of a busy day.

The BEANS absorb their fill of CHOW! Then it's time to digest and sleep.

They settle down to snooze beneath the spreading arms of their great spiritual guardian, GRAN'MA'PA.

YAWN...

Suddenly, in the middle of the night!

FIZ! FIZ! FIZ! FIZ! FIZ! FIZ! FIZ!

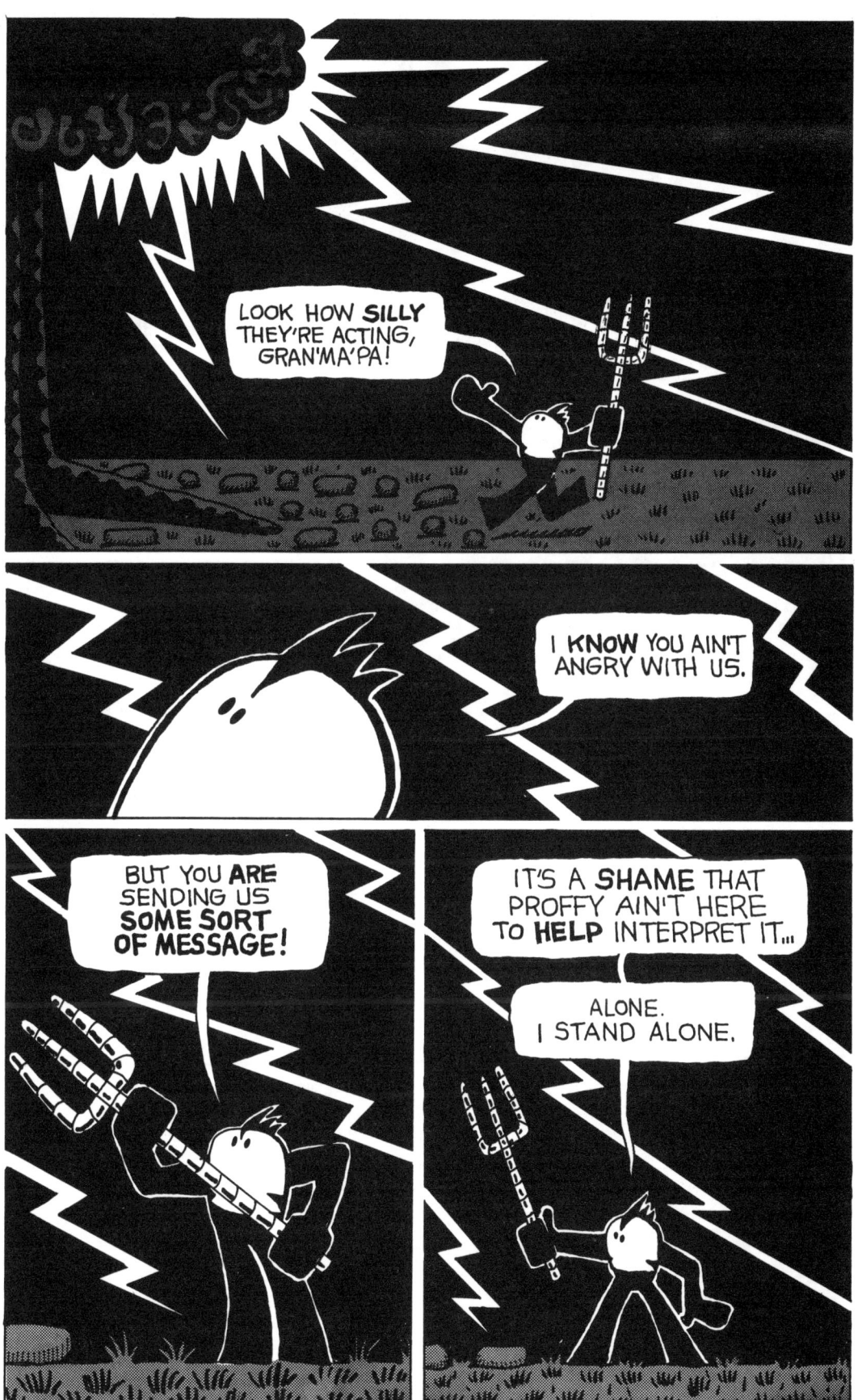

BEANISH WOULD ENJOY LOOKING AT THE REFLECTIONS OF LIGHT AND DARKNESS ON MY TRUSTY FORK.

ALONE. I GAZE ALONE.

THE BOOM'R BAND IS MISSING THE WILD FLASHING RHYTHMS OF GRAN'MA'PA'S LIGHT!

ALONE. I DANCE ALONE.

MR. SPOOK dances all night!

Right before dawn the flashing lights stop.

GEE, THANKS, GRAN'MA'PA. THAT WAS REALLY **FUN!**

In the morning...

C'MON OUT, YOU **COWARDS**!

NOK NOK

IS IT SAFE OUTSIDE?

SEEMS OKAY.

I CALL FOR AN IMMEDIATE COUNCIL MEETING.

YOU MISSED AN **IMPORTANT MESSAGE** FROM OUR **SPONSOR**!

WHY WAS GRAN'MA'PA SO **ANGRY** WITH US?

WHAT DID WE DO TO SO **OUTRAGE** OUR SPIRITUAL GUARDIAN?

HAVE YOU ALL GONE **CRAZY**? GRAN'MA'PA **LOVES** US! GRAN'MA'PA WOULD **NEVER** DO **ANYTHING** TO UPSET US!

WHEN GRAN'MA'PA MOVES, SHAKES, FLASHES OR KA·BOOMS, IT'S OUR **SACRED DUTY** TO OBSERVE **EVERY** MOVEMENT. WE MUST SEARCH FOR THE **SECRETS** BEHIND **EVERY** MOTION.

WHAT **WAS** THE **MEANING** OF LAST NIGHT'S OUTBURST?

I DON'T KNOW!

YOU'RE THE BIG BRAIN **GENIUS** AROUND HERE!

I'M **SURE** GRAN'MA'PA WAS COUNTING ON **YOUR** **INTELLIGENCE** TO **INTERPRET** THE **SIGNALS** CORRECTLY.

BUT NOOOOOOOOOO...

...YOU WIMPS GOT **SCARED** AND **MISSED** IT!

At the same time---directly above them.

THE NOCTURNAL TRANSMISSION REQUESTING SERVICE CAME FROM **DIRECTLY BELOW.**

I WANT EVERYONE TO APOLOGIZE TO GRAN'MA'PA FOR BEING SO INCONSIDERATE.

GREETINGS, CUSTOMER! ARE YOU **READY** FOR US TO **FILL** YOUR **LOADING DOCKS?**

OKAY?

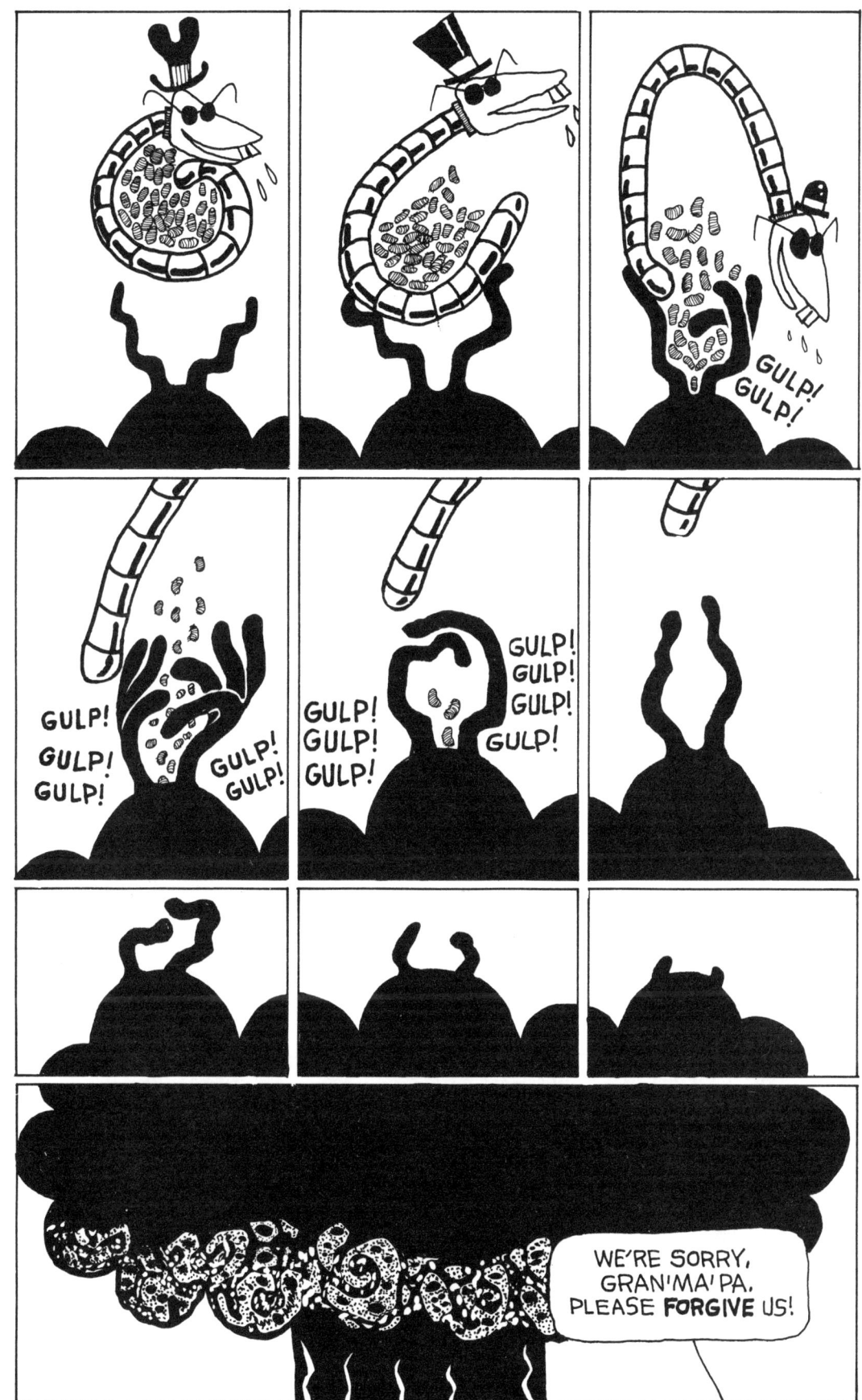

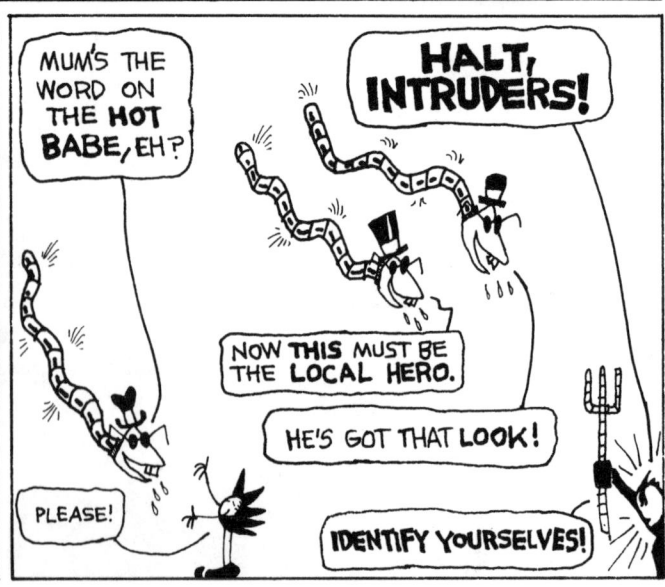

30

WE'ZE THE **GOOFY SERVICE JERKS!**

WHAT'S YOUR BUSINESS IN THE BEANWORLD

THE **HERO'S** PACKING A MEAN LOOKING **FORK!**

WE'ZE JUST ABSOLUTELY POSITIVELY DELIVERED A **FULL MEASURE** OF **REPRODUCTIVE PROPELLANT.** AS REQUESTED.

WE DIDN'T MAKE NO REQUEST.

NOT YOU!

WE'ZE GOT OUR CALL LAST NIGHT FROM THE TALL DARK, SILENT SENTIENT **BEHIND** YOU!

YOU?

GRAN'MA'PA WAS CALLING **YOU?**

OH YEAH!

I THOUGHT GRAN'MA'PA WAS SENDING **US** A MESSAGE.

NAW!

SAAAY, WHERE'D A **BUMPKIN HERO** LIKE **YOU** GET THAT **FORK?**

THE BIG-FISH-IN-THE-SKY **GAVE** IT TO ME AS A **REWARD!***

*TOTB#3

31

32

Golden. Gleaming. Wriggly rhythms.
Swooping. Soaring. Doo-wop harmony.

They chant it over and over, "A gift! A gift comes!"
At midday they depart. The singing fades in the distance,
but the **beans** keep the song going.

GRAN'MA'PA'S GONNA GIVE US A PRESENT!

A GIFT! A GIFT COMES!

A GIFT! A GIFT COMES!

IT'S ALMOST TIME...

I GOTTA GET TO THE SKETCH!

BOING

HELLO, BEANISH.

HOW ARE YOU TODAY?

LAST NIGHT GRAN'MA'PA **EXPLODED!**

OH MY!

WE THOUGHT IT WAS **THE END!**

THEN TODAY, THOSE **GOOFY SERVICE JERKS** APPEARED.

DIDN'T I ASK YOU NOT TO MENTION **THEM** AGAIN!!

YEAH... BUT... THEY WERE **BABBLING** STUFF ABOUT A **GIFT** FROM **GRAN'MA'PA...**

ARE THEY **DANGEROUS?** WHO **ARE** THOSE JERKS?

...OH MY...

YOU'RE **QUITE UP SET,** AREN'T YOU, BEANISH.

YES!

I'M SORRY I SNAPPED AT YOU!

DON'T WORRY ABOUT THE GOOFY SERVICE JERKS. THEY **TALK** BIG BUT THEY'RE JUST A SILLY **DELIVERY ORGANIZATION!**

WHAT DO THEY DELIVER?

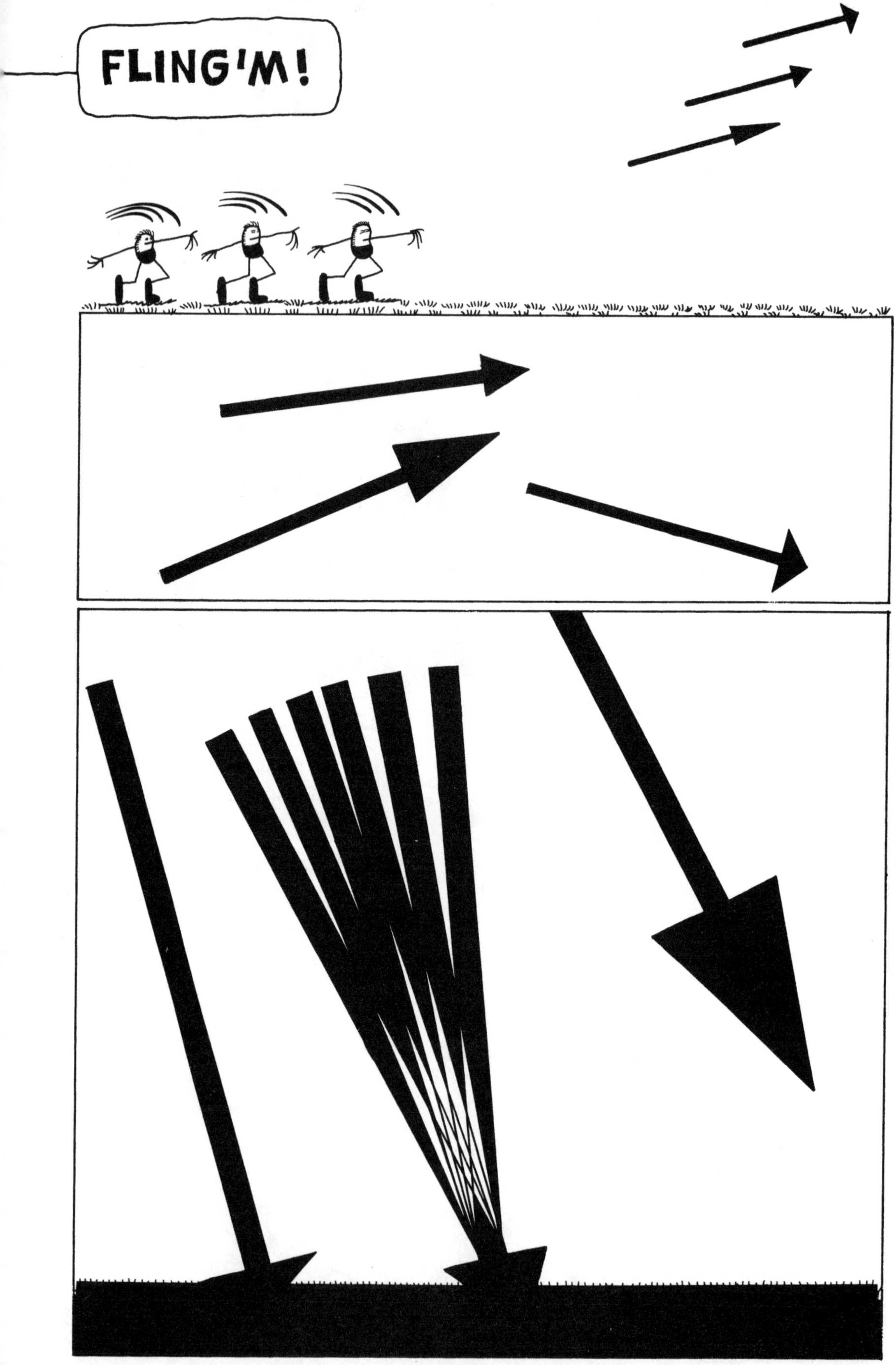

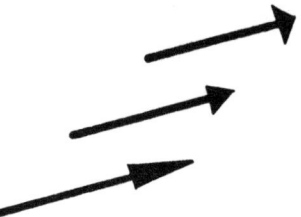

FLING'M!

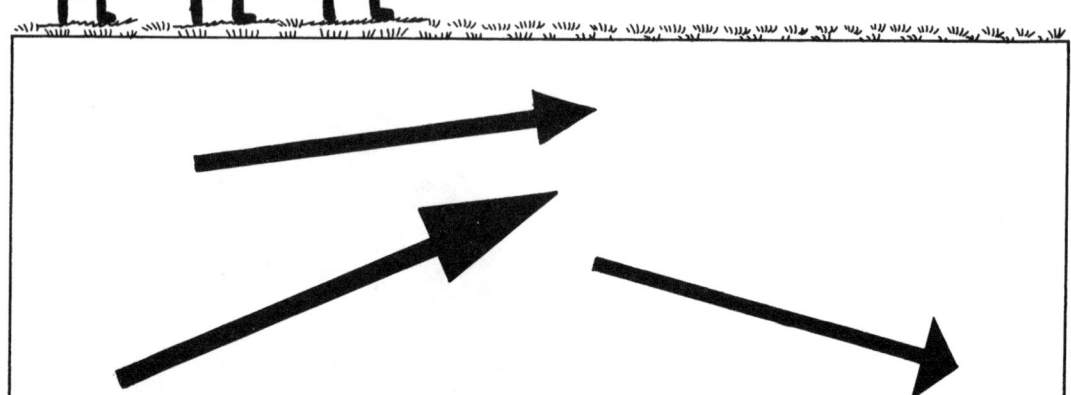

LET'S **FETCH'M**, SOL'JERS!

HEYYYY, WAIT FOR ME!

PREEESENT THE BALLISTICS STATISTICS, SOL'JERS!

HOO!

HOO!

HA!

Three differently shaped **CHIPS** mounted on **SLATS** of identical length and width.

TRAVELLED **FASTER** BUT NOT AS **FAR** AS THE STANDARD SPEAR.

THE STANDARD SPEAR.

TRAVELLED **FARTHER** BUT NOT AS **FAST** AS THE STANDARD SPEAR.

WHAT'S YOUR PRIMARY GOAL, MR. SPOOK: **SPEED OR DISTANCE?**

OUR NEW OFFENSIVE TACTICS WILL REQUIRE **DISTANCE**, PROFFY!*

*As shown last issue.

39

BEANISH is busy creating the FABULOUS LOOK·SEE·SHOW!

THIS "PROFFY" COMPOSITION LACKS **EXCITMENT**! IT'S TOO TOO **BALANCED**!

I'LL FIX IT WITH SOME **EXTRA FLOAT FACTOR**.

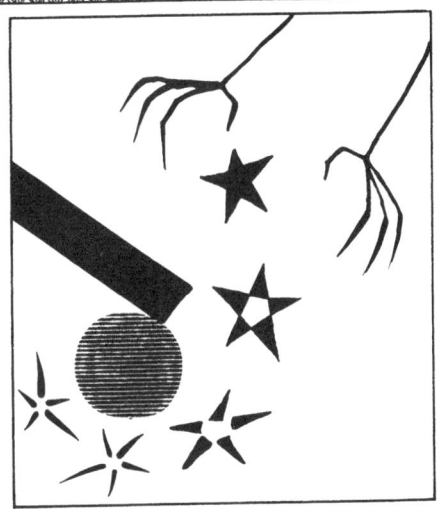

Much better!

I GOTTA GET **GOING**! IT'S ALMOST TIME TO VISIT MY **SECRET FRIEND**!

Everyday, at midday, **BEANISH** stands inside the "secret sketch" and travels to an unknown territory where he meets a secret friend.

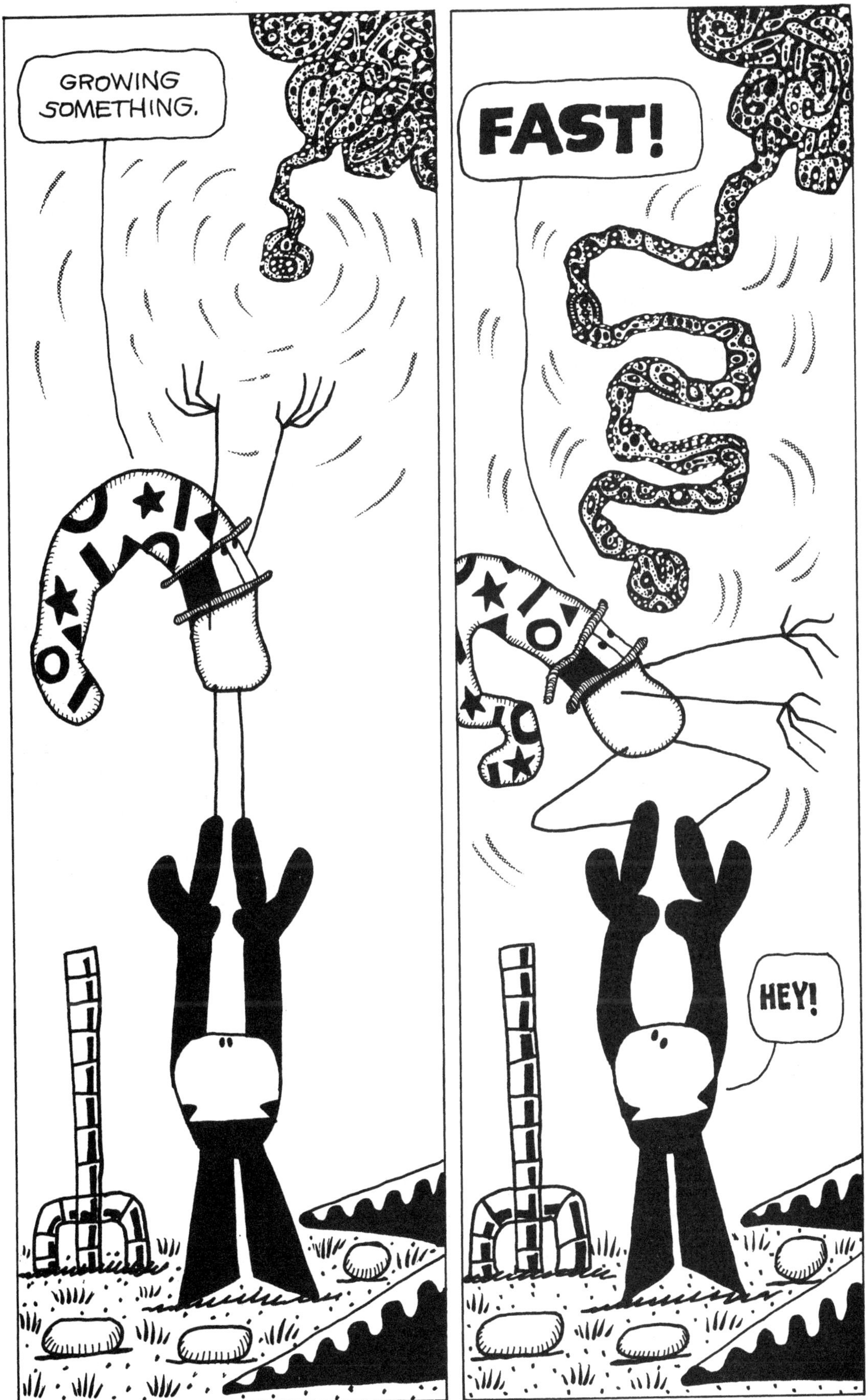
GROWING SOMETHING.
FAST!
HEY!

WOOPS!

Meanwhile, BEANISH makes last minute adjustments to his latest creation.

EVERYTHING'S READY!

It's time to gather the audience!

IT'S SHOWTIME!

49

A thorough search reveals:

NOTHING IN STOCK.

I'LL HAVE TO MAKE A TRIP TO THE FOUR REALITIES.

TWING!

I WISH I HAD TIME TO PURSUE THE **MYSTERIES** OF THE **FLOAT FACTOR** BUT IT'S MY **DUTY** TO DEVELOP A LONG DISTANCE SPEAR BEFORE I RETURN TO MY RESEARCH. THE **SAFETY** OF THE CHOW SOL'JERS IS MORE **URGENT!**

TOO BAD MR. SPOOK IS UNAVAILABLE FOR THIS **CHIP HUNT.** HE'S SO GOOD AT FINDING THE RIGHT SHAPE AND SIZE.

MAYBE I'LL BUMP INTO **BEANISH** AND **HE'LL** JOIN ME ON THE **HUNT.**

BEANISH has spent the morning staring at the big bulb!

IT'S GETTING **BIGGER** AND **FATTER**. WHAT'S THE DEAL WITH THIS **THING** ANYWAY?

It's almost midday.

I CAN'T MISS MY **APPOINTMENT!**

57

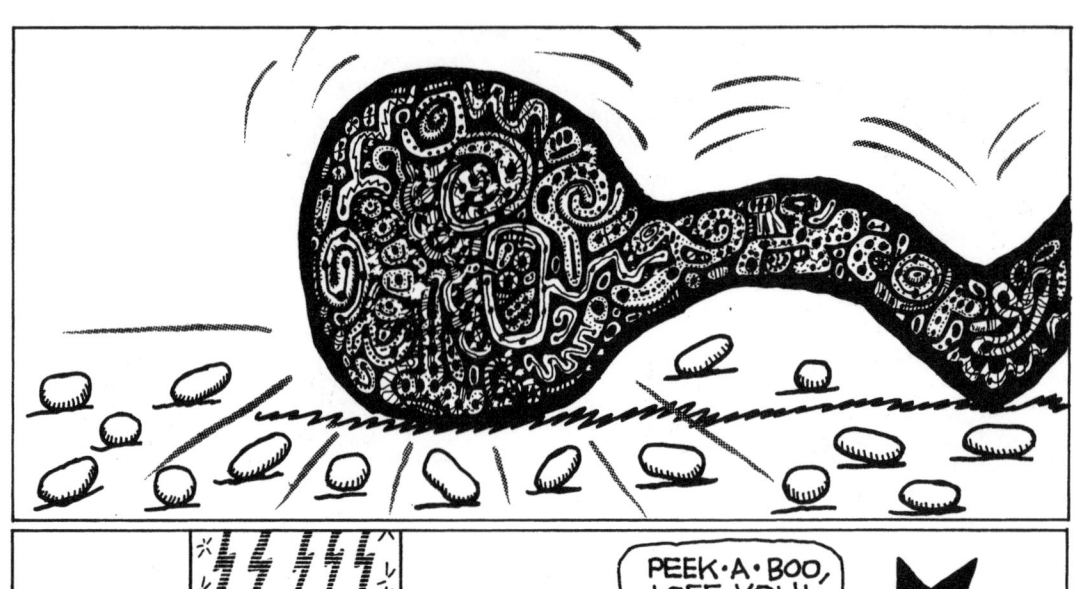

PEEK·A·BOO, I SEE YOU!

HI...

DID THE GIFT ARRIVE YET?

GRAN'MA'PA IS **DANGLING** A **STRANGE** CLUE BUT I CAN'T **SOLVE** THE PUZZLE!

WHAT ARE YOU TRYING TO **SAY**?

BEANISH explains.

SOUNDS LIKE A **HEALTHY GESTATION REPORT** TO ME!

ARE YOU SPEAKING THE SAME LANGUAGE AS ME?

OF **COURSE** I AM! YOU'RE JUST **NOT** GRASPING **ALL** THE CONCEPTS.

PLEASE TEACH ME.

59

They jump over the
LEGENDARY EDGE.

SPLASH!

SLATS

Slowly they
sink through
the FOUR
REALITIES.

HOOPS

TWINKS

I THINK I KNOW
WHERE TO FIND
SOME THAT SIZE,
PROFFY.

CHIPS

LEAD ON,
MY FRIEND!

THIS **IS** A
GOOD SPOT,
BEANISH.

A FLAT SLAT
SERVES AS
A CONVENIENT
TRAY.

HEY, LOOK! IT'S THE
CHOW SOL'JERS!

THEIR PLUK'IN WANDS ARE
BULGING WITH FRESH CHOW!

I'M GETTING HUNGRY.

ME TOO.

It's time to head for home.

The day ends with all the BEANS relaxing and feeding in the CHOWDOWN POOL.

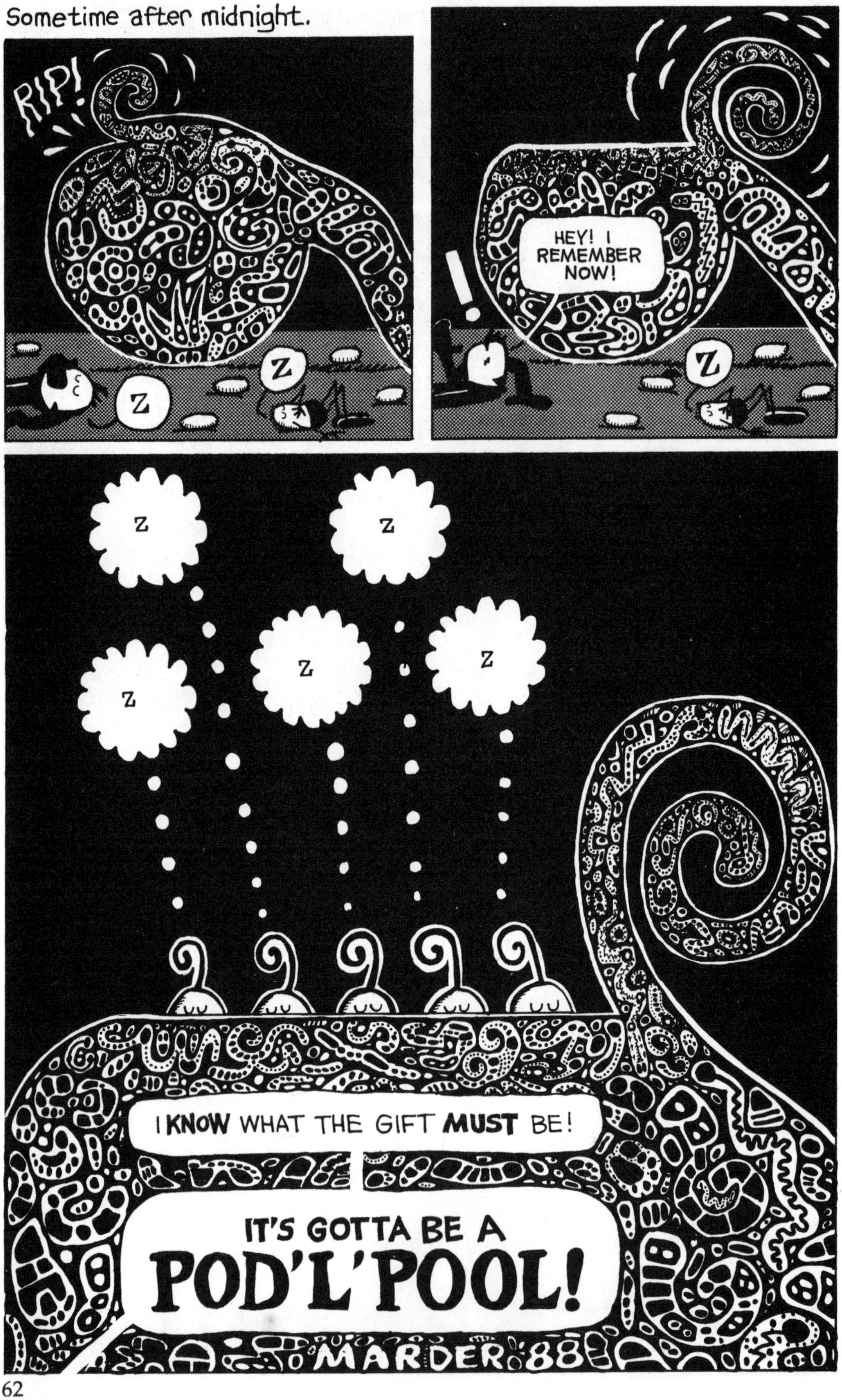

Sometime after midnight.

I **KNOW** WHAT THE GIFT **MUST** BE!

IT'S GOTTA BE A
POD'L'POOL!

MARDER '88

POD'L'POOL PAST.
POD'L'POOL PRESENT.

It's nightime.

The BEANS are snoozing beneath their spiritual guardian, GRAN'MA'PA!

MR. SPOOK is dreaming.

The world is CHOW! Warm, soupy and oh-so-delicious.

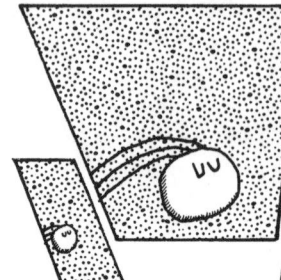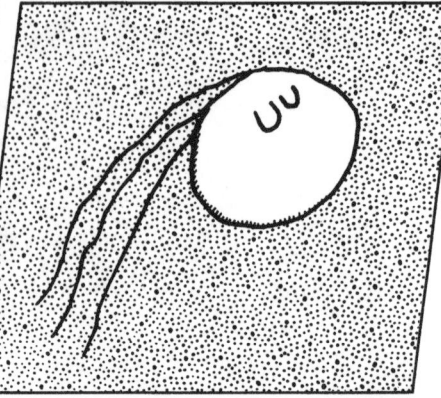

In a dazy, doze he **drifts** up and up.

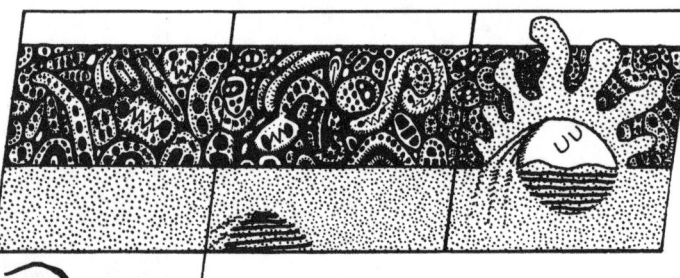

The cold air is a shockeroo! In his dream, MR. SPOOK snaps awake!

LONG TIME NO SEE, EH, **LITTLE HERO?**

Daybreak!

GOOD MORNING, BEANWORLD!

IT'S TIME TO RISE 'N' SHINE!

GOOD MORNING.

GOOD MORNING.

GOOD MORNING, FLANK'R.

PROFFY, WE'D LIKE TO FIELD TEST THAT LONG-RANGE SPEAR WE TRIED YESTERDAY.*

* Last issue.

Every morning MR. SPOOK assesses GRAN'MA'PA for the day's agenda.

HMMM.

I **DO** BELIEVE A SPROUT-BUTT **WILL** FALL TODAY.

IF I HURRY I CAN MANUFACTURE SOME TEST SPEARS FOR TODAY'S **ACTION**!

GREAT!

The CHOW SOL'JERS dance while they wait for the SPROUT-BUTT to drop. Suddenly, one of the BEANS notices the GIFT has had another shape shift.

HEY!

70

LOOK, MR. SPOOK!

SPROUT-BUTT ABOUT TO SHAKE ITSELF LOOSE!

A SPROUT-BUTT is serious business!

HURRY, HERO!

POP!

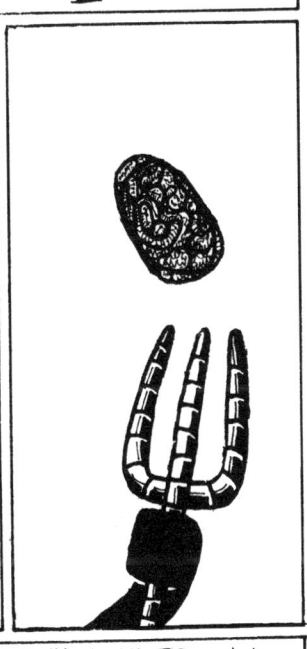

SNAGGED ME ONDA FOIST BOUNCE! IT'S GONNA BE YER LUCKY DAY!

SPROUT-BUTT, IS THE GIFT SOMETHING CALLED A POD'L'POOL?

TAKES ME TO DEM HANDSOME HUNKS, DA HOI-POLLOI, AND I'LL ANSWER UPON DELIVERY!

SPEAR FLING'N FLANK'RS rush to PROFESSOR GARBANZO'S FIX-IT SHOP to get the new weapons.

I WAS ABLE TO MAKE ONE TEST SPEAR FOR EACH OF YOU!

71

While the CHOW SOL'JERS seek war work, the others reason together.

SO WHAT DO **YOU** MAKE OF THE SITUATION, BEANISH?

I'M IN A JAM!

I D-DON'T, uh, KNOW WHAT THESE THINGS ARE, BOOM'R.

Actually he does.
His secret friend told him.

BABY BEANS.

BUT...

...I'M NOT ALLOWED TO REVEAL **ANYTHING** I LEARN AT OUR SECRET MEETINGS...

IF YOU BETRAY A CONFIDENCE, YOU WILL NEVER, EVER SEE ME AGAIN.

IT'S **SOOOOO** FRUSTRATING TO KNOW SOMETHING AND **NOT** BE ABLE TO SHARE!

WHAT'S UP THERE, BEANISH?

I DUNNO... HAVE A LOOK FOR YOURSELF.

?

It looks like MR. SPOOK has found a good war.

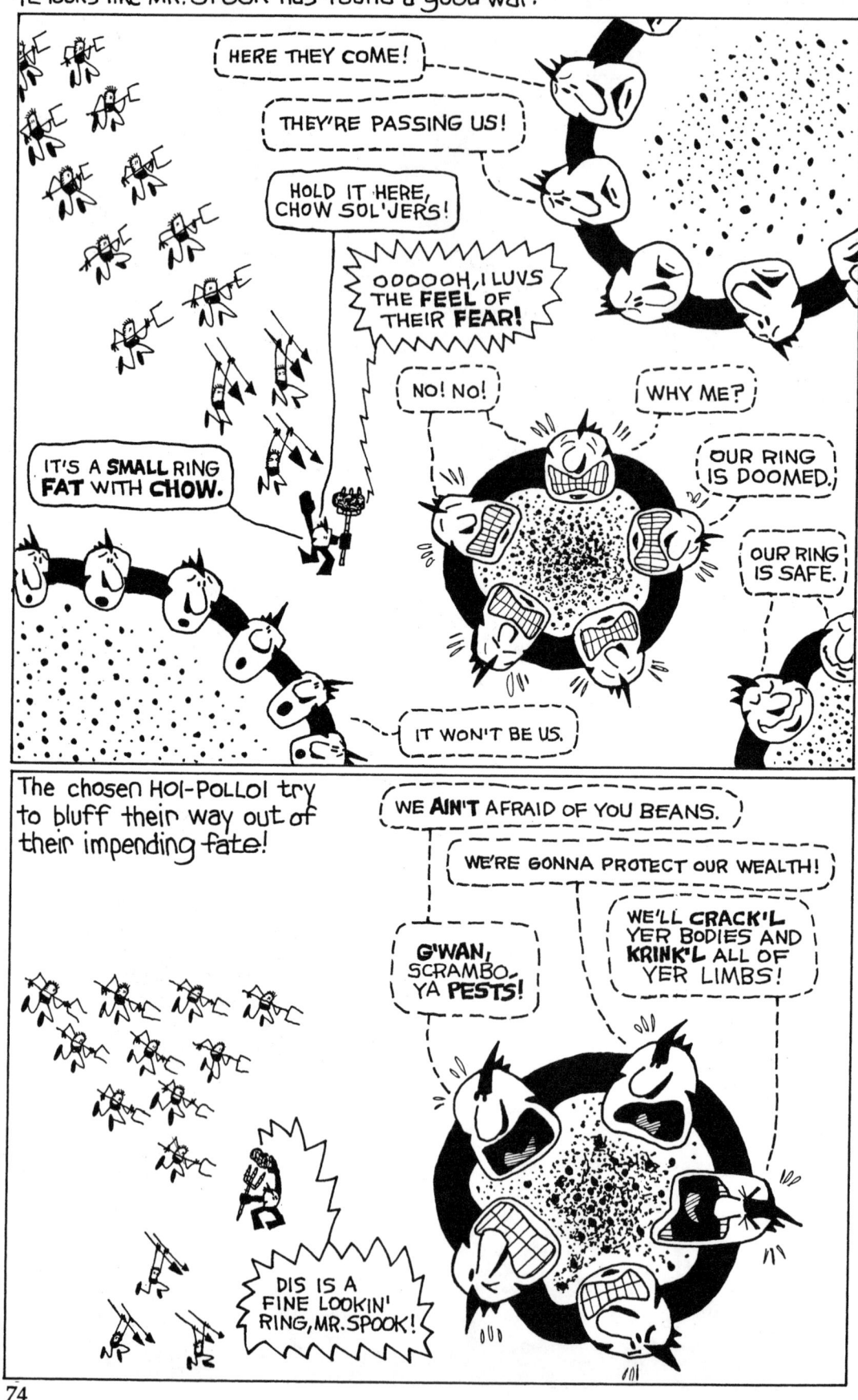

74

This is a tense moment.

WE'LL **CRUSH** YOU CRIMINALS!

I HOPE THEY DON'T GRAB **ME** TODAY!

LET'S FLING THE EXPERIMENTAL SPEARS FIRST.

The strategy is simple: ENRAGE and SEPARATE!
Physical abuse forces the HOI-POLLOI to forget their
primary impulse: TOTAL CHOW PROTECTION!

The SPROUT-BUTT is hurled. The combat begins.

YOW!

WHEE!

BONK!

NO, DON'T LET GO! **STAY IN RING FORMATION!**

PROTECT THE CHOW!

The CHOW PLUK'RS line up in a wedge near the break in the HOI-POLLOI RING.

THEY'RE SNEAKING UP BEHIND US!!

AW, NO!

The SPEAR FLING'N FLANK'RS' job is to enlarge the break.

FLING'M, FLANK'RS!

The experimental long-distance SPEARS fly.

75

It's a **WILD FLING!**

OOPS!

LOOK OUT!

OH, NO! THE SPEARS OVERSHOT THE TARGET HOI-POLLOI.

I DON'T BELIEVE IT! THEY MISSED ME!

THIS IS AWFUL!

This is an opportunity for the HOI-POLLOI.

LOOK, WE CAN **CLOSE** THE HOLE, FORM A SMALLER RING AND KEEP **OUR** CHOW SAFE.

YEAH.

WHAT TH'-?

WE'RE GONNA LOSE THE CHOW!

WE GOTTA KEEP THE BREAK BROKEN!

IT'LL NEVER WORK

YOU DON'T HAVE ENOUGH TIME, BEAN!

THE RING IS CLOSING!

MR. SPOOK is a HERO. He's always in the right place at the right time!

SEE WHAT LUCKINESS YA GOT WHEN YA SNAGGED ME ONDA FOIST BOUNCE, TODAY!

POW!

HOO·HOO·HA!

HOKA·HOKA·HEY!

NO!

HURRY! HURRY!

Meanwhile, back at the GIFT...

It's almost midday.

I GOTTA GET TO THE SKETCH!

Anxiety becomes anticipation.

Everyday at midday, BEANISH stands inside his SECRET SKETCH and travels to an unknown territory where he meets his friend.

BOING!

Here he can speak freely.

WE FOUND'EM!

DON'T I EVEN GET A NICE "HELLO"?

OOOPS... SORRY... HELLO.

WE FOUND THE BABY BEANS.

Will she tell?

*TOTB #6

TOMORROW WE TALK **NAMES!**

BOING!

BOING!

Back at the CHOW RAID.

THOSE BUMS STOLE OUR CHOW AND BEAT US UP.

WE'RE BROKE!

Nothing hurts more than that FRESH·OUT·OF·CHOW feeling.

MR. SPOOK fetches the SPROUT-BUTT.

HURRY UP, MR. SPOOK, DEY NEED **ME** NOW!

I'VE KEPT **MY** HALF OF THE BARGAIN! NOW TELL ME, IS GRAN'MA'PA'S GIFT A POD'L' POOL?

YEP! SURE IS!

NOW IT'S TIME TO DO SOME REMEDIAL **RESTORATION!**

HOI-POLLOI pain and misery arouses the SPROUT-BUTT's natural urges.

POP!

This ignites a lusty emotion called SPROUT-BUTT FEVER.

81

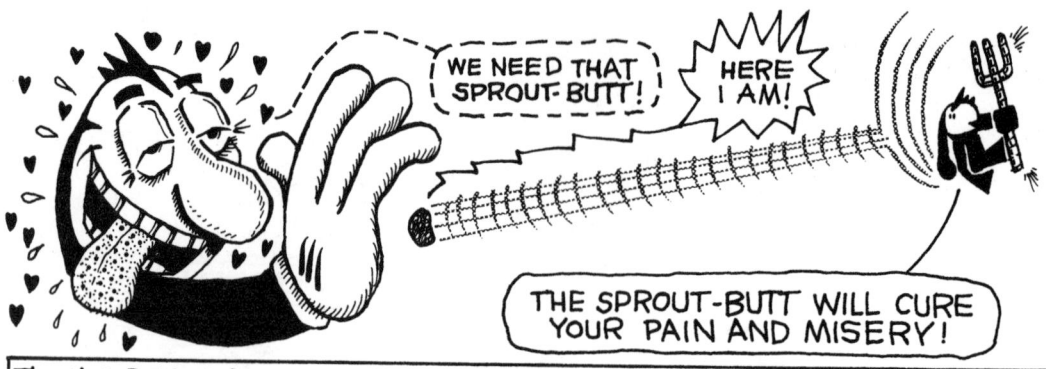

The HOI-POLLOI form a RING around the SPROUT-BUTT and croon!

The SPROUT-BUTT will be so overwhelmed with LOVE that it will:

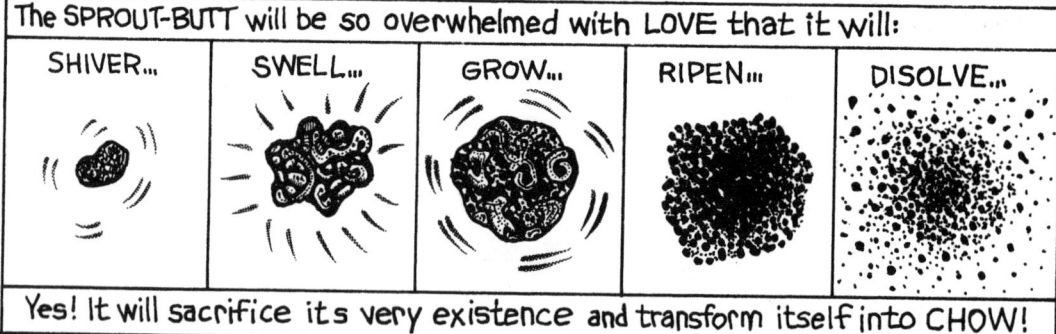

SHIVER...   SWELL...   GROW...   RIPEN...   DISOLVE...

Yes! It will sacrifice its very existence and transform itself into CHOW!

Then the HOI-POLLOI will split the CHOW and resume their crazed gambling.

OF COURSE, SOME DAY, WE'LL RETURN AND STEAL ALL THE CHOW AGAIN.

NATURALLY, WE'LL LEAVE ANOTHER SPROUT-BUTT!

THE LIFE GRAN'MA'PA PROVIDES IS PERFECT AS LONG AS WE ALL CARRY OUT OUR DUTIES.

The next morning.
MR. SPOOK assesses
GRAN'MA'PA for
the daily agenda.

NO SPROUT-BUTT
WILL FALL TODAY!

It's a **GOOF-OFF DAY**— a time for rest and relaxation from the stress
of CHOW SOL'JERING. Normally there is dancing and game playing. Today,
the only thing anyone wants to do is get a glimpse of the GIFT.

WHAT DO THEY
LOOK LIKE?

I CAN
HARDLY
WAIT.

HURRY IT
UP, SISTER.

THE VIEW
MUST BE
WORTH THE
WAIT!

I WISH I
GOT IN LINE
EARLIER.

C'MON SIS, TIMES UP!

AWWWWWW.

THEY'RE
SOOOOO
CUUUUTE

BEANISH's mind is elsewhere.

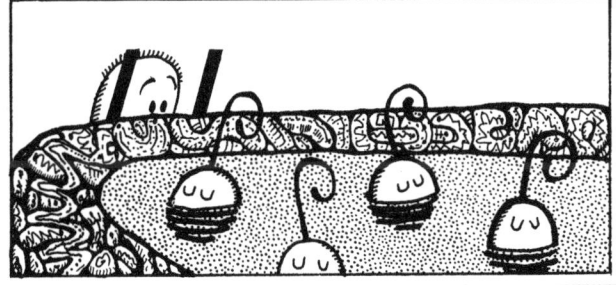

TODAY!

BOING!   BOING!

TODAY.

TODAY
WHAT?

UH OH.

UH ... TODAY'S FABULOUS LOOK·SEE·SHOW IS
CANCELLED DUE TO, UH, **THE GIFT!**

IT'S CALLED
A POD'L' POOL.

WHAT?

HOW DO YOU KNOW THAT?

MR. SPOOK explains.

BUT I DIDN'T HAVE NO DREAM LAST NIGHT.

BEANISH rudely walks away without saying goodbye.

I DON'T BELIEVE IT!

WHAT'S WITH HIM?

MR. SPOOK HAS **ALL** THE **SECRET INFORMATION** I HAVE! PLUS HE'S ALLOWED TO **TALK** ABOUT IT!

I DON'T THINK I'LL **EVER** UNDERSTAND THAT BEAN.

WHAT'S THE USE OF HAVING INFORMATION IF YOU **CAN'T** PASS IT ALONG?

WHY DOES MY FRIEND **TEST** ME IN THIS WAY?

WILL MY FRIEND **REALLY** REVEAL A NAME TODAY?

OR WILL IT BE ANOTHER **AGONIZING TEST**?

The wait is over.

DO NOT SPEAK!

I AM BUT A CRUDE SKETCH IN THE BIGBIG PICTURE. MY POWER IS WEAK BECAUSE I AM SMALL.

I AM SMALL BECAUSE I AM INCOMPLETE, UNFINISHED, IN NEED OF **SOMETHING MORE!**

SO I ASK: SHALL I CONTINUE TO BE YOUR RAVISHING RADIANT **KNOT** OF **PERPLEXITY?**

ARE YOU **STRONG** ENOUGH TO **ENDURE** THE **STRUGGLE** OF **TRUE LOVE** AND **DEVOTION?**

ARE YOU **SMART** ENOUGH TO **TRANSLATE** THE **SIGNALS** INSIDE THE **SPLENDOR** AND **RAPTURE?**

WILL **YOU** HELP **ME** IN **MY** ATTEMPT TO BE "**SOMETHING MORE**"?

SHHH, DON'T ANSWER NOW! THINK IT OVER, GIVE ME YOUR ANSWER **TOMORROW.**

TOMORROW.

ALWAYS TOMORROW...

WHAT **WONDERS** AND **TRIALS** LIE ON THE OTHER SIDE OF A "**YES**"?

89

Night.

Morning reveals...

Everyone's at the POD'L'POOL.

91

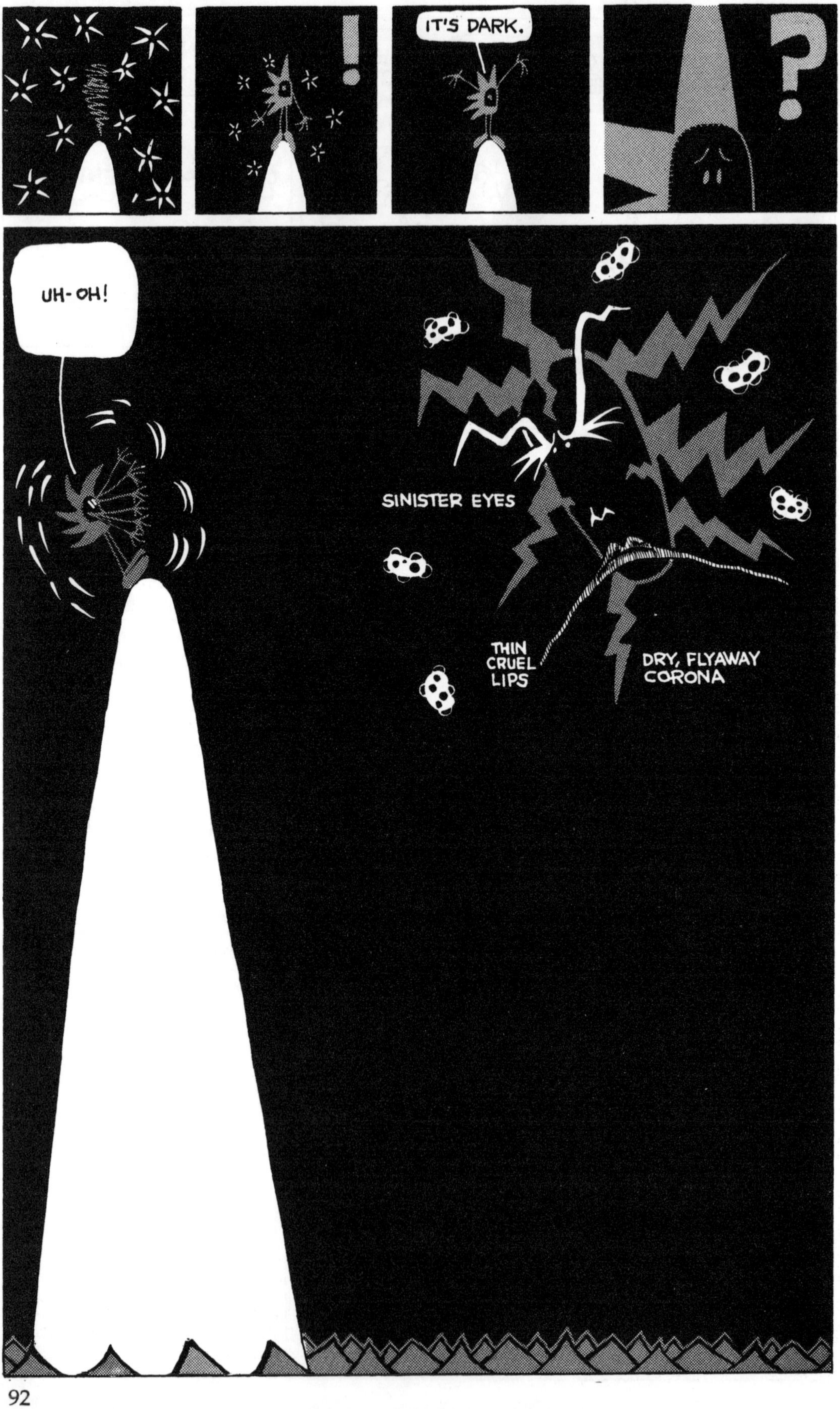

Notworm Madness!

NO! AN UGLY LITTLE MERCILESS MONSTROSITY!

THEY'ZE MERCILESS MONSTROSITIES AROUND HERE?

WE'ZE BEST GET OUTA HERE!

UH-OH!

WHICH WAY TO THE NEAREST EXIT, PAL?

THAT·A·WAY!

WE'ZE ON OUR WAY!

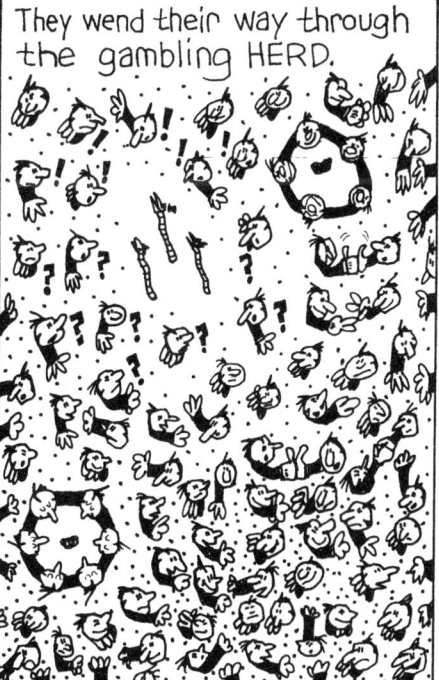

They wend their way through the gambling HERD.

ALRIIIIIGHTY! A CHANGE OF SPACE!

WHERE ARE WE'ZE NOW?

IT'S A PROVERBIAL SANDY BEACH!

WE'ZE FOUND A FAMILIAR TERRITORIALITY!

SURE! WE'ZE DOWNLOADED REPRODUCTIVE PROPELLANT HERE RECENTLY!*

WE'ZE GOTTA SEE IF THE CUSTOMER IS FULLY SATISFIED!

The BEANS are in line to view the POD'L'POOL CUTIES.

C'MON, PROFFY! HURRY IT UP!

YOU'VE LOOKED LONG ENOUGH!

AWWW....

TURN'S OVER!

DON'T BE SELFISH!

* See TOTB No 8.

98

Here come the **GOOFY SERVICE JERKS!**
GREETINGS, CUSTOMER.
HOW GROWS THE GIFT OF LIFE?
C'MON, MR. SPOOK, QUIT STALLING!
LET US HAVE A TURN
AWWW...
GET DOWN FROM THERE!
HERE'S THE PROGRESS!
WE'ZE BEST RUN A GOOFY SERVICE ☑ CHEK!®

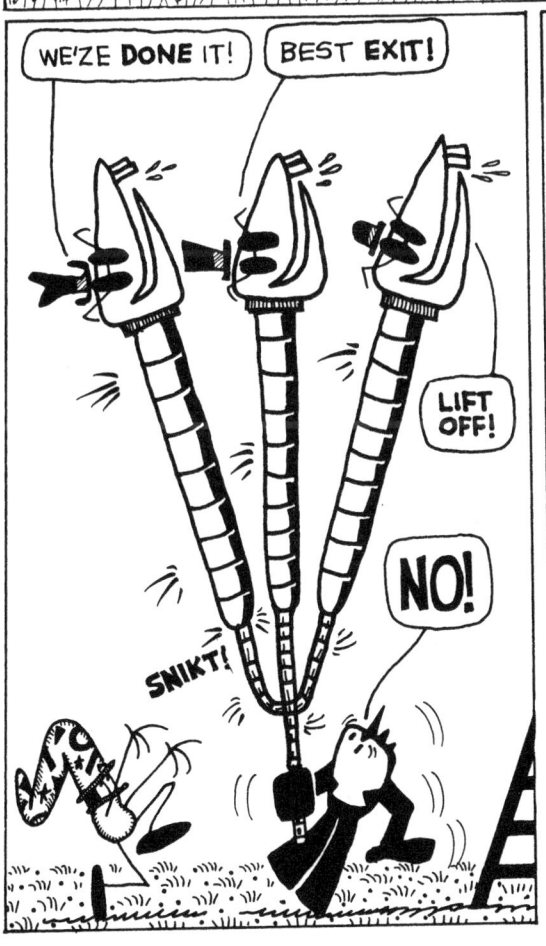

103

105

It's a long, long way down.

107

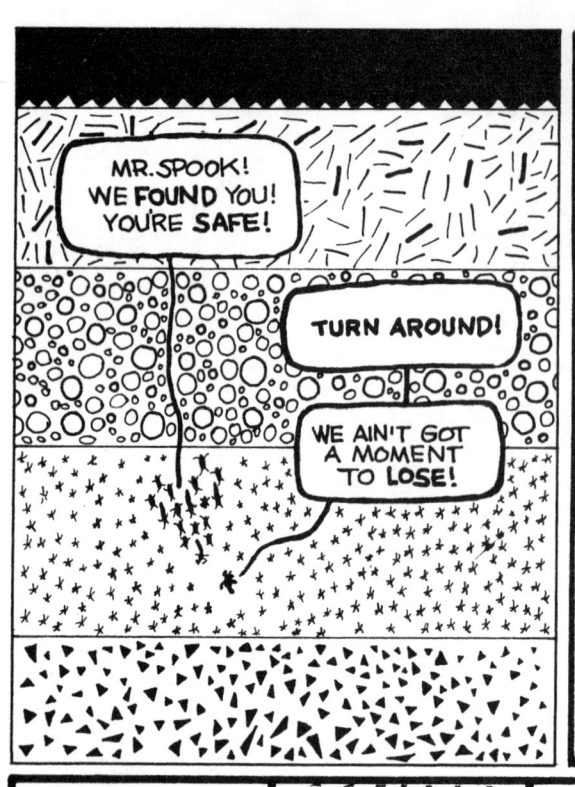

You may recall that BEANISH spent the morning **lost** in deep **thought**!*

THE **DEMANDS** OF **SECRECY** ARE A **HEAVY BURDEN**...

Oblivious.

SHOULD I SAY "YES"?

* Last issue.

I'M GONNA SAY "YES"!

TOTAL ECLIPSE

!

IT'S DARK.

?

MY FRIEND, WHAT'S **HAPPENED** TO YOU?

gibberish!

WHAT ARE YOU **SAYING?** I CAN'T **UNDERSTAND** YOU!

111

BEANISH is back!

113

IN THE END WE WERE ABLE TO PUT EVERYTHING BACK TO NORMAL. IT WAS KIND OF COMPLICATED.

I THINK YOU MAY HAVE VENTURED BEYOND THE **FRAME** OF THE **BIG·BIG·PICTURE**!

YOU ACTUALLY STEPPED **OUTSIDE** OF THE **CONTINUITY**!

YOU'VE HAD AN EXPERIENCE EVEN **I** CAN'T IMAGINE.

I DID IT TO HELP **YOU**!

YOU ARE **INDEED** A **WORTHY FRIEND**.

HER VOICE FILLS ME WITH A COZY WARMTH!

NOW, I MUST DEPART, BUT THERE IS **STILL** TIME FOR YOUR REPLY TO YESTERDAY'S QUESTION.

YESTERDAY?

IT'S STILL TODAY??

I FEEL LIKE I'VE BEEN AWAY FOR A **LOOOOONG** TIME!

BEANISH?

HOW IS THAT POSSIBLE?

BEEEEEEANISH! THE QUESTION!!

QUESTION?   OH, YEAH... SORRY.

I'LL **SUFFER** ANY HARDSHIP, CONFRONT ANY CALAMITY IN ANY PLACE OR TIME IN ORDER TO HELP YOU HELP YOURSELF BE "SOMETHING MORE."
(or something like that.....)

YES!
MY ANSWER IS
YES!

I KNEW YOU'D AGREE!

SEE YOU TOMORROW. I WANT TO KNOW MORE ABOUT THIS ADVENTURE YOU WENT ON.

TOMORROW.

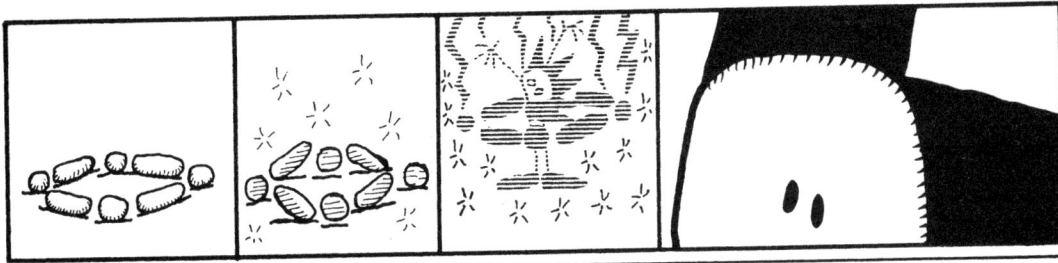

I **NOW** KNOW THINGS **DREAMISHNESS DOESN'T** KNOW??

COULD THIS HAVE BEEN A **HIDDEN** PURPOSE FOR MY **ADVENTURING?**

IT WASN'T JUST A **TEST!** NOW I HAVE SOMETHING TO BRING TO OUR **DAILY CONVERGENCE!**

STARTING **TOMORROW,** AS SHE TEACHES **ME,** I'LL HAVE STUFF TO TEACH **HER** TOO!

UNTIL THEN I GUESS I'LL GET IN THE LINE TO VIEW THE **POD'L' POOL CUTIES.**

WE GOTTA **HURRY** AND MAKE SURE THE **POD'L' POOL CUTIES** ARE **NOT** IN **DANGER!**

HEY?!? WHERE'D THE LINE GO?

ARE THE BABY BEANS STILL HERE?

HERE THEY ARE.

AWWWW...

YOO HOO, BEANISH!

THE CUTIES ARE THE **BEANS OF THE FUTURE.**

WE ALL SHARE THE **RESPONSIBILITY** OF TEACHING THEM TO GROW UP PROPERLY!

I WUZ HOPIN'TA SPEND **LOTS** OF TIME WITH'EM **MYSELF,** Y'KNOW?

BUT I GOTTA DO SOMETHING ELSE **FIRST!**

TAP! TAP!

O GRAN'MA'PA, HEAR MY CRYING!

I SWEAR BY THE **MEMORY** OF MY **TRUSTY FORK** TO **AVENGE** ITS **SENSELESS DEATH,** EVEN IF IT TAKES ME EVERY DAY OF **THE REST OF MY LIFE!!**

NOTWORM MADNESS!

I'M HUNGRY.

118

Hoo•Hoo•HAs & a Hoka•Hoka HEY!

A few words from the creator of Beanworld

LARRY MARDER

DEDICATION EXPLANATION

When I was growing up, my family lived in the northern suburbs of Chicago perched on the edge of Lake Michigan. Chicago is a beautiful place, sometimes, and other times... well... the weather stinks. Really bad weather meant playing inside all day. In the 60s, children stuck in the house had few entertainment options—no cable, no VCRs, no electronic games. There were only four television stations, and during the day, three of them might be airing soap operas or something equally boring to a couple of housebound boys, in this case, my little brother Jonny and me.

Jonny and I invented a whole slew of games, some were clever and some were dumb. But there was one game we played that is relevant to *Beanworld* in general and to this volume specifically. It was *"The Bugs Bunny Game."* Or rather, it was *"The Let's Design A Cool House For Bugs Bunny Game."*

Our Dad put up a blackboard for us and we played the game on the board with chalk. We would jointly design and I would carefully draw very elaborate under-the-ground homes for Bugs Bunny. These drawings were elaborate cutaway diagrams displaying all the various rooms and the connecting tunnels and passageways. Where this idea came from is lost in the fuzziness of the past, and Jonny is no longer with us, so I can't ask him what he remembers, or even know for certain if he'd even remember the game, but I'm telling you, I certainly do.

As far as I can piece it together, the germ of the idea probably came from two places. The first being the Bugs Bunny and other Warner Brothers cartoons we regularly watched on WGN. The idea that Bugs had a vast underground estate perhaps was communicated in a cartoon or two. I'm not an expert on these things, but I do have a vague memory of something like that. The idea of diagramming it had to have come from comic books—cutaway diagrams of Superman's Fortress of Solitude or the Batcave were things we would have certainly been aware of.

As we grew up, I can't say I spent any time reminiscing about this childish indoor activity, but as I designed Professor Garbanzo's Fix-It-Shop, the memories of the game came welling up, nearly overwhelming me.

My brother was only three years younger than me. He was an amazing kid with an awesome sense of humor. To me, one of his greatest skills was stringing together nonsense words and sounds in tantalizing patterns and phrases. I learned how to do this from him. Take my word for it, if he hadn't been my brother for 19 years, I would never have developed the ear that allows me to manufacture words like Gran'Ma'Pa, Pod'l'pool or Gunk'l'dunk.

He's been gone twenty three years now and I still think of him every day, but sometimes, when I'm working on *Beanworld,* I swear he's looking over my shoulder whispering *"It's called Tu'Ba'Lu Squiberish."*

THE LONG AND SILLY STORY OF TOTAL ECLIPSE

Some rather odd, seemingly inexplicable events occur between pages 110 and 114 in this book during the eclipse sequences. This is because the story makes several references to a long forgotten comic book mega-event called "Total Eclipse."

As you may recall, in 1984, the husband and wife team of Dean Mullaney, Publisher and cat yronwode, Editor-in-Chief, of Eclipse Comics "discovered" me and *Beanworld*. We became good friends and *Beanworld* joined their publishing family alongside Scott McCloud's *Zot!*, Tim Truman's *Scout* and Doug Moench's *Aztec Ace.* At the time,

Eclipse was a real contender for the number three slot in the publisher's race for market share. At any given moment Eclipse was either third, fourth, or fifth largest publisher of comics books after the mega-giants Marvel and DC Comics. In 1988, they decided to celebrate their tenth anniversary of publishing comics with a major event. The idea was that every character that had ever made any sort of appearance in an Eclipse Comic would appear in an extravaganza called "Total Eclipse"

I was asked, along with dozens of other creators/writers/artists to loan out some of my characters and/or concepts for this publishing event. When Eclipse first approached me about this, no one on either side had any intention of genuinely inserting *Beanworld* into the "Total Eclipse" concept. My initial reaction was to just have the Beans making a brief cameo in the background or perhaps having one of the *DNAgents* or *Zot* reading a *Beanworld* comic or some other sort of equally silly cop-out.

Then the press release announcing Beanworld's participation in "Total Eclipse" was sent out. You should have heard the howling! It stirred up a hornet's nest of emotions. I received hate mail for the first time. The general reaction was:
a) *Larry Marder has lost his mind*
b) *Eclipse was somehow forcing Larry Marder to "sell out"*
c) *both of the above*
The answer, of course, was
d) *None of the above*
As the ramifications of what I had stirred up were becoming more apparent on a seemingly daily basis, I realized what an opportunity Eclipse had handed me. That *Beanworld* would participate in something so commercial was absolutely appalling, not only to my fans, but to the entire comic book community.

What a terrific challenge! And I was really up for it too. The question was *"How can I participate in "Total Eclipse" and still maintain 100% of Beanworld's hard won integrity and respect?"*
Everyone at Eclipse assumed I would want to showcase Mr. Spook, because it was generally agreed he was the most popular Beanworld character. I said *"Forget Mr. Spook. Think about Beanish and Dreamishness."* I explained that I had plotted and planned an "eclipse of the sun goddess" sequence

years before and was planning to insert it into the storyline at some point in the distant future. My plan was for Dreamishness to go dark, become cruel and speak gibberish. I knew that this sequence would represent an extremely important part of the Dreamishness/Beanish relationship. It was no trouble at all to move it forward to accommodate the "Total Eclipse" storyline without compromising myself in any way, shape or form.
So I did. That was the easy part.
My idea was that the Dreamishness would "eclipse out" and while having a dialogue with Beanish, Aztec Ace would poke up his head from the Thin Lake, wrap his fingers around Beanish's island/mountain/ whatever that thing he stands on is and silently, unnoticed, observe the Beanworld characters and think *"This is a most peculiar reality,"* and then sink back down under the water. There would be no character interaction, there would be nothing added or subtracted to the *Beanworld* continuity. This was agreed upon by both myself andcat yronwode.

But no one had gotten around to telling "Total Eclipse" writer, Marv Wolfman. So when the script of "Total Eclipse" came in, it had a page long *Beanworld* eclipse sequence in it starring Mr. Spook. cat knew it was outside of our agreement, but because it was written, she decided to show it to me. In the scene Marv wrote, the everyday *Beanworld* sun (not Dreamishness) goes into eclipse turning day into night and the Beans are overwhelmed with primitive panic and fear. Mr. Spook stays calm and instructs the Spear Fling'n Flank'rs to hurl their spears at what ever is hurting the sun! It was really cute but it was totally wrong. It wasn't ***my*** *Beanworld*. I told cat so. She told me we could drop the scene, or if I wanted to, it was fine with Marv if I wrote my own.

I recognized that inserting an "eclipsing sequence" into the *Beanworld* continuity offered me a great opportunity to tie up a few of my own loose ends. While writing "A gift! A gift comes" I realized that I was getting mighty sick and tired of having to write around the obstacle of Beanish not knowing if his friend was a he or a she. It was time for the sun character to reveal her secret name and ask Beanish "The Big Question." But in between her question and his answer I desired for Beanish to have an intense, daz-

Marv Wolfman wrote and Bo Hampton drew Total Eclipse. I drew my own characters but I wasn't allowed to letter their dialogue except for Dreamishness' gibberish balloons. Compare this frame from Total Eclipse with the same sequence on page 110 of this volume.

This frame showing Beanish in Miracleman's hand was my favorite single image in Total Eclipse.

zling, shamanistic experience that would knock him silly! *But what kind of experience should it be?*

In the real world, a shaman is a person of extraordinary power. The power is often a result of a spiritual visitor from another world, dimension or reality. The visitor can appear in a dream or a vision, sometimes in human form, sometimes as an animal, sometimes something elemental like a whirlwind or an earthquake, even sometimes in a surrealist form like a burning bush. Often the person is taken to another world and confronted with sickness and/or death. Often the spiritual visitor gives the person a sacred word or object. Sometimes instructions are given on how to find or build a sacred fetish or medicine bundle. If the person is able to survive his/her ordeal, he/she returns home with much to ponder and contemplate. In fact, the rest of the person's life is governed and influenced by the vision experience. The person is now a shaman. Shamanistic powers usually enhance the ability to hunt, wage war or heal sickness.

Well, the answer to my question *"What kind of shamanistic experience should Beanish have"* was right there in front of me! I could combine the name/question sequence in such a way that would allow Beanish to leave the world of the Beans—to actually leave and go outside of its continuity. He was transported to "a separate reality," was brave, did what was asked of him and came home knowing far more than when he left. As I wrote at the time, "After all, from Beanish's point of view, what could be more unworldly *(more unBEANWORLDly)* than one of those super-hero series where everyone teams up to fight some omniversal Hitler."

That was when I decided to let the two continuities intermingle a little. Instead of the usual comic book "crossover," I came up with the idea of a "cross-through." The two continuities would intersect. I wrote and drew a brief sequence that would appear in both *Beanworld* and "Total Eclipse" simultaneously but independently. The *Beanworld* version appears on pages 92 and 110-112 of this book. And in keeping with my desire for this to be a shamanistic experience, I decided that Beanish must not suffer comic book amnesia and forget his experiences in the world of magic and science. In Beanworld, we would learn of Beanish's adventures in the way he remembered having them. And that is the way it has played out ever since.

One last note. It had always been my intention that when this collection was published, that I would retell the entire "Total Eclipse" story from Beanish's point-of-view. Since then, Eclipse collapsed into bankruptcy and all the rights got entangled and ensnarled in legalities. Except for its importance as a "crossthrough" in *Beanworld* continuity, the Eclipse mini-series is all but forgotten. Personally I have lost "total interest" in "Total Eclipse." At this point, we should let the dead rest in peace.

THE GOOFY SERVICE JERKS

I'm not really sure when I came up with the idea of the Goofy Service Jerks. The notion of a celestial messenger who delivers the baby Beans *after* something disturbing occurs in the night was part of my story from as far back as its very beginnings. It is very clearly demonstrated in the two following sequences from 1983-4.

The first is an attempt at a pencil breakdown for a chapter of the *Beanworld* freezine. Since 1976, I'd been toying with a story that would begin with an individual Bean suffering from insomnia and subsequently stumbling onto an esoteric secret. Insomnia is a subject near (and not so dear) to my heart. I often suffer from it (believe me, at Image Comics enough bizarre things happen on a semi-regular basis) causing me to be wide awake in the middle of the night. The announcer/messenger/fertilizer is a kachina headed character. This particular character eventually ended up evolving into Mr. Teach'm. The sequence contains the refrain "A gift. A gift comes."

The second sequence I find far more interesting. This breakdown contains Beanish and Dreamishness' first meeting sequence that eventually ended up in *Beanworld #5* in a story titled "The Float Factor."

By then, I had abandoned the notion of a single kachina-headed character in favor of a trio of goofy announcer/messenger/fertilizers. I tinkered with these characters over many months. My original intention was that the group of announcers be the insect-like creature team of Uncle Xaspa and his nephews. I even hinted at this in the inside back cover of *Beanworld #6*. I really love those li'l insects. I used them in several of my non-Beanworld oriented cartoons that were in the 3 issues of my self-published 'zine *Heyoka* in 1983-4. But when I arrived at this part of the Beanworld story, they didn't seem to fit right, so I knew I had to develop some new ones. This breakdown, rendered in marker, showcases the transition between Uncle Xaspa and the Goofy Service Jerks. I include both as historical curiosities.

Larry Marder
Newport Coast, CA
November, 1997

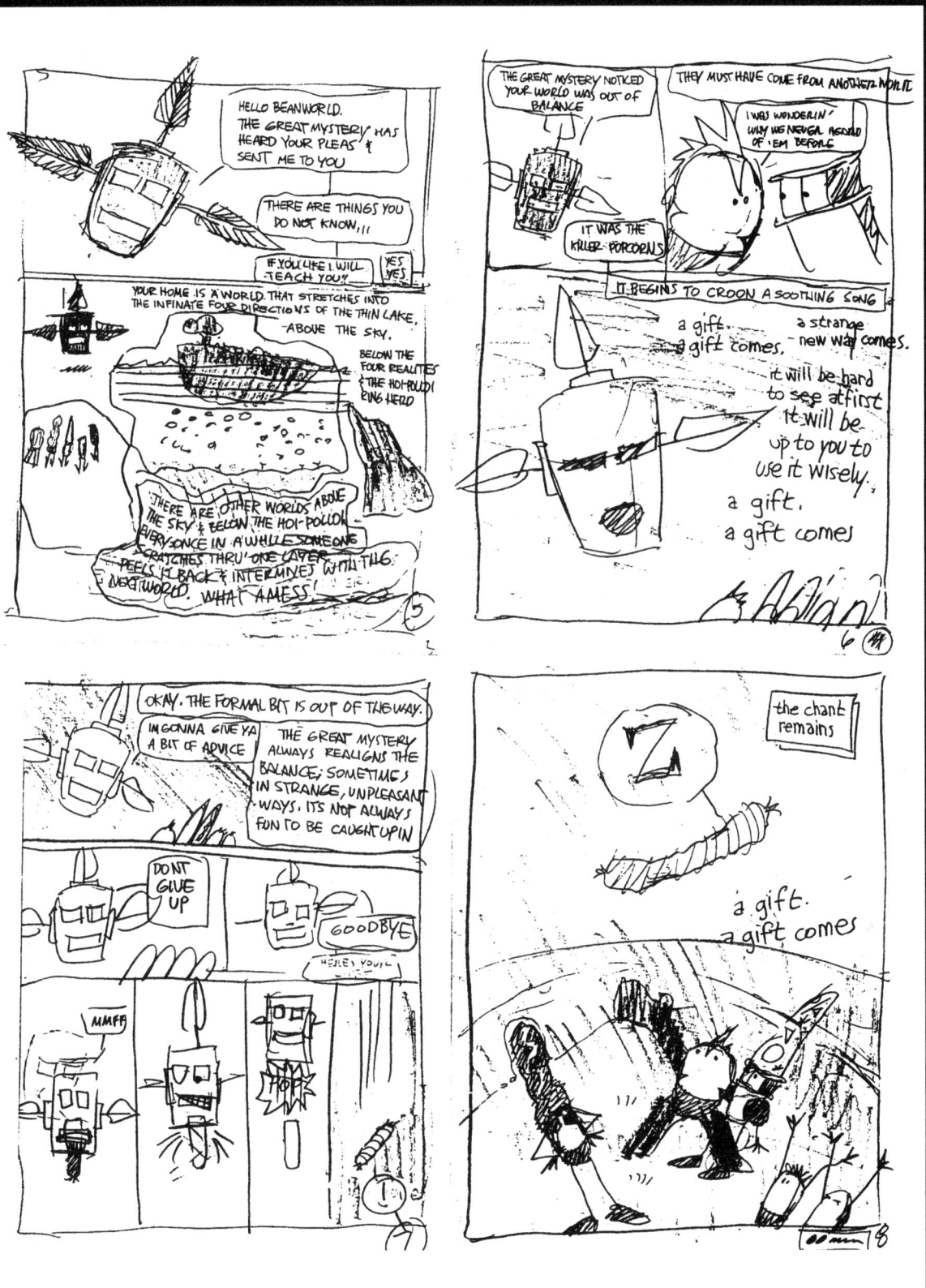

That NIGHT Gran'Ma'Pa THUNDER STORMS !!!

IT'S UNANIMOUS !!!

The MYSTERY PODS are INFESTICATION AIGS!!

TWINKS function as a natural insecticide. Each AIG (or mystery pod as you so quaintly refer to them) is rendered UNHATCHABLE when it is CHANGED by contact with TWINKS.

That solves ONE PROBLEM and creates another. 'Floatus Fluxis™' has its own potential problems.

Do you understand anything I've just said?

soaring 3 part harmonies

YOU HAVE A NEW POWER
NEW POWER NEEDS NEW IDEAS
NEW IDEAS NEED NEW MINDS
NEW MINDS MEAN NEW BEANS !!!

OKAY. THE JOB IS DONE and EVERYTHING IS FIXED!!

AND LOOK, IT'S REALLY VERY IMPORTANT THAT YOU KNOCK-OUT THOSE INFESTIGATION AIGS!

KEEP WORKING ON TWINKS NO MATTER WHAT!

DON'T YOU TRY TO STOP EM EITHER!

Ok

MR. SPOOKS HANDS'LL BE FULL OF OTHER PROBLEMS SOON ENOUGH... HA HA

and the MAINTAINANCE CREW SPLITS!

art MAKER

I'LL TRY THAT OLD IDEA I NEVER DID WITH THIS

I'LL JUST STEP IN & PLACE THIS SLAT--

ZIP-ZAP! BEANISH IS GONE, THE PODS ARE ON THE GROUND & THE TWINKS ARE GONE!! ALSO!!

WILD'N' WAKY WAHOOLAZUMA!!

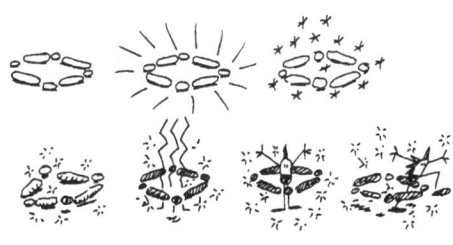

Beanish rushes off to tell someone, ANYONE about hiz CRAZY adventure but what he finds stops him cold...!!!

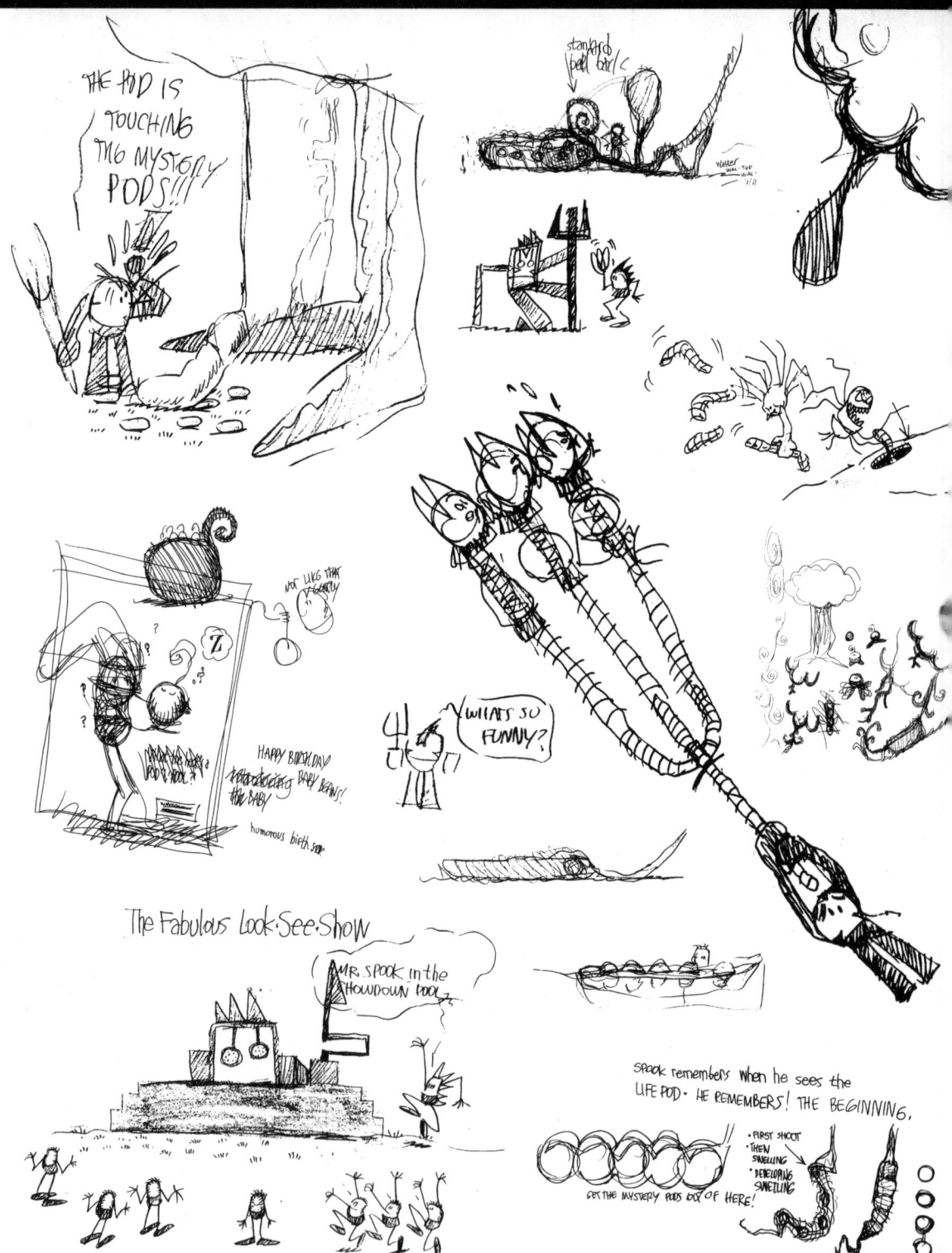

Any drawing that I create while being paid to do something else I call a Goofy Service Doodle. All the sketches on this page were drawn during client meetings circa 1986-8 when I was a creative director at a Chicago advertising agency. In those days I often spent hours and hours in marathon meetings where the client would drone on and on about the merits of his product. Often I'd zone out and start solving Beanworld problems on the pages where I was supposed to be taking meeting notes.